THE SPHINX STRIKES

H. BEDFORD-JONES

THE SPHINX STRIKES

H. BEDFORD-JONES

ALTUS PRESS • 2015

EDITED AND DESIGNED BY
Matthew Moring

PUBLISHING HISTORY

"Spy Against Europe" originally appeared in the February 23, 1935 issue of *Argosy* magazine (Vol. 253 No. 5). Copyright © 1935 by The Frank A. Munsey Company. Copyright renewed © 1962 and assigned to Steeger Properties, LLC. All rights reserved.

"Free-Lance Spy" originally appeared in the March 30, 1935 issue of *Argosy* magazine (Vol. 254 No. 4). Copyright © 1935 by The Frank A. Munsey Company. Copyright renewed © 1962 and assigned to Steeger Properties, LLC. All rights reserved.

"The Sphinx Strikes" originally appeared in the May 18, 1935 issue of *Argosy* magazine (Vol. 255 No. 5). Copyright © 1935 by The Frank A. Munsey Company. Copyright renewed © 1962 and assigned to Steeger Properties, LLC. All rights reserved.

THANKS TO
Joel Frieman, Everard P. Digges LaTouche and Gerd Pircher

TABLE OF CONTENTS

I

SPY AGAINST EUROPE

In this most dangerous game, The Sphinx, iron-nerved spy, was instructed—"Suspect everybody! And remember, murder is nothing in this business."

CHAPTER I

DOUBLE-CROSSING RATS

WHEN JOHN BARNES stepped aboard the Imperial Airways plane at Croyden field, he was taking his life in his hand, and knew it. When he stepped out of the plane at Le Bourget and got into the bus headed for downtown Paris, Death was chuckling at his ear. His one chance was that nobody suspected what he was doing.

Back in London, just before he left, the American ambassador had made things quite clear.

"It's a new deal all around, Barnes, at home and abroad. We're fighting these Europeans with their own weapons for a change. Remember, you've no earthly connection with Washington! You and the other chaps in the game are taking your chances— long chances, Barnes. You're devoting your time, money, and lives to a cause. You'll have no reward except the satisfaction of serving your country. If you're caught—goodnight!"

"Thanks," Barnes said laconically. "Instructions?"

The ambassador handed him an envelope. "Here. Chew up the paper and destroy it before you land at Le Bourget. This assassination of King Boris and the other in Marseilles has turned things upside down; vital information is en route to us, and it must reach Washington at once. There's a leak in the Paris embassy; we can't trust it. If you can get the message here—well, it's up to you."

Aboard the plane, Barnes memorized his instructions. With them he found a list of eight secret agents who had been caught

From the back
of Sheldon's neck
protruded the haft
of a long knife.

and killed within the past month. None were Americans, but the grim significance of this list was obvious. Barnes knew Europe. He had lived abroad for several years. He had been in business in Paris. Level-eyed, quiet, seldom losing his head, Barnes was no Herculean figure; that was how he got results. Few people suspected his capabilities.

That other men, like himself, were unofficially serving their country, that he had been drawn into a free-lance game against all Europe, was great news. As the bus headed along the cobbled, ugly streets of Paris slipped past. Barnes stared out at them unseeing, his mind active, racing.

A new deal, now! America, unofficially, was taking a hand in the game. The very thought held a tang of adventure. No dirty spy stuff; that was barred. Europe was back in prewar days now. Intrigue, suspicion, assassination, war trembling on every frontier; a secret, merciless war going on beneath the surface. Barnes had caught echoes of it here and there; he knew what he was heading into. A new deal, eh? Yes, European diplomacy was going to get a hot jolt.

His primary instructions were simple. He was to go to the Hotel Dupont in the Rue du Selz and there await from Sheldon some word, which might come in an hour or a week. Sheldon was trying to get out of Belgrade, which was no easy matter. If he reached Paris alive, he would no doubt be trailed and shadowed.

"Then it's my job to get the information, whatever it is, out of France," Barnes reflected. "But the Dupont! Why pick on that joint, of all places?"

He knew the Hotel Dupont by reputation, which was bad. The little downtown hostelry was no better than a house of assignation. To anyone who knew Paris, the place had an evil stench. However, orders were orders.

Upon reaching the bus terminal at the Crillon, Barnes picked up his one small bag, which was little more than a brief-case, and set out afoot for his destination. He did not know Sheldon; a former newspaper correspondent, who had become the mainspring of America's new initiative against the massed intrigues of Europe. He had a full description of Sheldon, however, and could not mistake his man.

Barnes sauntered along the narrow little Rue du Selz. Gone were the old gay dollar-grabbing days when tourists had flooded Paris. Now the shops looked dingier, the prices were down, only French faces appeared in the streets. Paris was still staggering under depression and the resentment of unpaid national debts.

There was the old Dupont. A mere entry way between two store fronts. Pushing into the place, Barnes found himself in a narrow little hall; a desk on one side, an elevator on the other, a flight of stairs in the rear. At the desk was a man, swarthy, sharp-eyed, who folded up a newspaper and rose.

"Good morning," Barnes greeted him in French. "I'd like a room, a double room. It's just possible that I shall have company later. With bath."

The other beamed. "All things can be arranged, *m'sieu*. A fine chamber on the third is vacant. Fifty francs."

Barnes protested this price, which was presently cut to forty. He filled out the police registration slip; as instructed in his orders, he gave the name of John Smithson. The police, he knew, would not bother to check up on his identity unless some trouble arose. And if this happened, Barnes intended to be gone before his real name could be involved and his passport impounded.

As he was finishing with the various blanks on the paper, a young woman descended the stairs and came to the desk, leaving her key. Barnes glanced up and thrilled to the sight of her face; dark and lovely, with eyes to hold a man in dreams. Those eyes dwelt upon him for an instant, and he fancied that a startled flame rose in them. Then she was gone out the doorway to the street.

"You are lucky, *m'sieu!*" and the greasy proprietor winked at Barnes. "*M'amselle* Nicolas is also on the third—eh, eh, what is this? *Tiens, tiens!* Smeethson—name of a little black dog! *M'sieu*, there was a gentleman here inquiring for one of this name, not twenty minutes ago. He would soon return, he said."

"When he returns, send him straight up to my room, if you please."

The other nodded and opened the elevator door. Barnes was taken up to the third—which, in America, would be the fourth. The ground floor is not counted in France. His room was comfortable enough. It had one window opening on a little iron balcony, and a makeshift bathroom, with all plumbing exposed, the pipes running along the wall.

Left alone, Barnes lit a cigarette and went to the window, which looked out on a court. Probably there were not twenty rooms in this whole "hotel," which was merely a slice from some ancient building, refinished and painted liberally.

"This is a devil of a hole in which to do any waiting," he mused. "But, since it must have been Sheldon who asked for me, I'll not have long to wait. I wonder why that girl gave me such a queer look? Nicolas, eh? Names mean nothing. She was a beauty, all right."

It was past noon; no wonder he felt hungry. A house telephone was on the wall. Barnes gave the proprietor a ring and ordered a meal. Then he began to pace up and down the room. Just what was he in for, anyway? He had not the least idea. Even the ambassador had not known.

ONLY SHELDON knew just what was up, it seemed. With a shrug, Barnes dismissed his pondering, threw open the window for air, and was tempted to step out on the balcony. He refrained, however. Best not to show himself there.

A waiter arrived with a folding table, spread out an excellent luncheon, and departed with his pay. Barnes drew up a chair, poured some wine, and pitched into his meal. He was nervous and uneasy. He had the distinct feel of something about to happen. His usual calm, his cheerful audacity, was darkened; his high spirits were dulled.

Suddenly came a sharp rap at the door. Before he could respond, the knob was turned.

The door opened and closed again, to admit a man. It was Sheldon; thin, red-haired, with a big nose. A man of forty. He looked at Barnes and grinned.

"Hello! So you got here, eh? I'm Sheldon. Had your description."

Barnes reached for the other's hand, eagerly.

"Barnes is the name—as you seem to know. Join me?"

"You bet. Grub looks good; I'm famished. Got here this morning and have been imagining things ever since. How soon can you clear out for London?"

"In five minutes."

Sheldon dropped into a chair, his back to the open window, and seized on a glass of wine.

"Not quite so fast, but almost, is necessary. You know what's up?"

"I know nothing," Barnes replied. The other was eating as he spoke.

"Hell of a mess. This murder of King Boris has precipitated no end of trouble; we don't know if it means war or what. I had to come via Germany, and couldn't get out. Barely got a plane before the Nazi pincers closed down. I expected they'd have spies waiting to meet me here, but nothing so far. Boy, I've got the goods!"

His blue eyes gleamed exultantly. From his pocket he drew a small but heavy brown envelope, most impressively sealed, which he tossed at Barnes.

"This is a fake, in case you're caught. It's a good fake, too." From his wrist he unbuckled a watch, which he passed over likewise. "Here's the real stuff; get it to the ambassador in London at all costs."

"This watch?" queried Barnes.

"Exactly. Never mind explanations; the less you know, the less you'll give away."

"Right," said Barnes. He gave Sheldon his own watch and buckled on the one given him; it was not running, he observed.

"We've got a hell of a big strike," Sheldon ejaculated between bites. "The lowdown straight out of Belgrade—secret treaties with Italy and so on. The less you know the better, I suppose."

"Who's against us in this deal?"

"Everybody," snapped Sheldon. "We've got what nobody else has, and what they're all after. Me, I'm all shot to pieces. My nerve's gone."

"Any special instructions?" Barnes demanded, pocketing the sealed envelope. Sheldon gave him a shrewd look.

"Yes. This is no kindergarten game we're in. These birds have their countries back of 'em; you and I don't. When you've been in it as long as I have, your nerves will go, too. Suspect everybody! And remember, murder is nothing in this business. They're on to me, all right, but let's hope you've not been spotted. I'll let 'em follow me, while you get across the Channel in a hurry."

"Right. How did you come to pick on this hotel?" queried Barnes.

"I know the chap who runs it; he's part-way straight. There's a hell of a fine girl here—the Nicolas girl. She's been working for Bulgaria, but somebody double-crossed her and I hear she's in Italian pay now. I believe she's in Rome at present."

"She was here when I entered," Barnes said. "The man at the desk called her by name. Very pretty, with dark eyes."

"What the devil! Then somebody lied to me—as usual," Sheldon exclaimed. "No matter. I've not slept for two nights. Lock the door, will you? I was warned they'd try to murder me; I haven't felt safe until now." Barnes went to the door and shot the bolt.

"Wouldn't you be safer in a big hotel like the Lutetia?"

"Nope. They probably know already that I'm here. You'd better be moving. Spare no expense; you may need this, take it." He flung on the table a big wad of various European currencies. "Get out to Le Bourget and hire a special plane; an English one."

"Thanks." Pocketing the money, Barnes began to pack up his few belongings. He went into the bathroom, getting his toilet things. "Who's your danger from?"

"All directions," came the voice of Sheldon. "We're safe enough from the English; they're not interested this time. Boy, with this information we can blow all the others high, wide and handsome! All these double-crossing rats!"

"Hope so." Barnes was packing his toilet articles. "Finish up the grub. I'll get some more at Le Bourget. The room's paid for, by the way."

A grunt from the other room made response.

Swiftly, Barnes repacked. He was in the game at last; elation filled him, all his depression was gone. Now he was alert, eager, tense.

Another half hour and he would be at the air field, then swiftly winging back to England!

"When I reach London, I'll send a wire, so you can take it easy," he called. Sheldon made no response. When he finished his packing, Barnes carried his little bag out into the other room. Then, abruptly, he came to a dead stop.

Sheldon had fallen over sideways in the chair, his head lolling. From the back of his neck protruded the haft of a long, heavy knife.

At this instant came a harsh, determined pounding on the door.

"In the name of the law, *m'sieu!*" came a stentorian voice. "Open!"

CHAPTER II

THE BROWN ENVELOPE

BARNES GLANCED swiftly about. Sheldon was dead; murdered a moment ago. One glance at that horribly lolling head told the tale. By whom? The room was empty. Ah—the open window, the balcony! Someone had been outside there—

And, in a flash, Barnes knew that this same balcony was his one hope of escape. He knew what threatened him and his precious burden. Let him be caught, accused of this crime, let the French have any handle by which to detain him, and his mission was ruined. It was his job to get through with that information—at all costs!

His hesitation lasted no more than ten seconds. His bag bore nothing to reveal his identity; he dropped it beside the dead Sheldon and darted to the window. There, to his surprise he found that the balcony was not merely confined to his own window, but ran around all the windows of the courtyard. Thus, anyone could go from one room to the others of this same floor. The balcony was now empty, however.

"Made to order for hotel rats, diplomats and assassins!"

Barnes thought grimly. A tremendous burst of hammering came from the door of his room. He stepped outside.

To tell whence the assassin had come, was impossible; the rooms to the left, however, would be closer to the stairway. Barnes turned left at a venture. A low cross-bar of iron, over which he stepped, and he was at the adjoining window. Closed and locked. He passed on. At the next, he found the door-like sash also closed. A splintering crash came from behind, a burst of voices; his room had been entered. A moment more, and he would be discovered here.

The window sagged under his hand. He pushed, threw his weight against it; the double sash flew open, and he staggered into the room.

To his vast relief, the chamber proved to be empty.

He closed and fastened the window again, then glanced around. The room was smaller than his own. Women's clothes were in sight. Could it be possible?

Was this the room of the Nicolas girl, which was on his own floor? With a shrug, he dismissed the thought, and stood listening.

The tumult of feet and voices continued. Realization of his own predicament grew upon Barnes with acute force. Smithson would certainly be accused of the murder. Should he walk downstairs now, at once, daring everything? Audacity, always audacity! So thinking, Barnes went to the door and reached for the knob.

At this instant, a key was inserted from the outside.

A laugh, a man's laugh, came clearly to him. The door was unlocked and thrown open, thrown back against Barnes as he slipped aside. It momentarily concealed his figure.

"Very well, I have kept my promise," said a woman's cool, poised voice. "You are in my room. Now clear out—and do it fast!"

"Bah! Don't play the fine lady with me. Shut the door and

be sensible," said the man, in a light and bantering tone. "What's all the commotion about?"

"I don't know and don't care," the woman replied. "Get out!"

A laugh, a heavy thudding slap—then the door was slammed shut and locked.

Against it stood the Nicolas girl, flushed, angry. For an instant she did not realize the presence of Barnes, who thus stood revealed. Then her eyes dilated in evident fear. Pallor flashed into her face. She shrank back a little against the door.

"So I was right!" she murmured in English. "When I saw you downstairs, I should have taken warning. I guessed that you must be the man—"

"Apparently you made a very good guess," Barnes said coolly. He was not the person to miss so obvious a cue. Next instant she drew herself up, her dark eyes ablaze.

"You dare not, you dare not touch me!" she exclaimed. "There are police in the building now; at a scream from me, they will come!

"What's more, Sheldon should be here at any moment; Sheldon, do you understand? This is France, my friend, and not Russia."

Barnes was startled. "So it is, Miss Nicolas. What is Sheldon to you?"

"Nothing. He is a friend, and an honest man. No assassin like yourself!"

"Be sensible. I've no intention of harming you," and Barnes smiled faintly. He was badly shaken by what had taken place. Above all, he was conscious of the hatred and fear straining in her eyes.

"Liar! You are trying to trick me, eh?" she said scornfully. "As though I didn't know they were sending you! As though I haven't been watching every day, every hour! Only, I expected it would be Borescu. Come, who are you?"

Barnes produced and lit a cigarette, with assumed composure.

HE WAS fascinated by her beauty—a perilous beauty. After what Sheldon had told him, he knew her for one of those magnificently alluring women who play an old, old game in Europe. What cause they serve, whose pay they take, to whom their reports go, remains obscure; except when one of them is stood against a wall and shot. And not bad women, either. Sheldon had said this was a fine girl, and Barnes could well believe it. Character and brains, not loose morals, are needed to play such a game as hers.

"You just mentioned a Rumanian name with which I am not familiar," Barnes said.

"Borescu? The murderer? Well, never mind evasion. Just who are you?"

"If I told you that," Barnes replied calmly, "you'd know far too much. In plain words, I'm not the person you take me for. I was hiding in this room."

"Nonsense. You even know my name."

"Certainly. Sheldon told me about you. He thought you were in Italy."

"Sheldon!" Her lovely eyes dilated again. "Then he is here?"

"Ten minutes ago, yes. He was murdered, two rooms from here."

Her features tightened; a flame of swift, passionate anger leaped in her eyes.

She believed in him, but she betrayed no shock, no grief. Evidently Sheldon had been nothing to her—nothing more than a friend.

"He was an honest man, that American. And you killed him?"

"No," said Barnes. "Why go into all this business of explaining? It takes too much time, and you'd not believe me anyway."

She regarded him steadily for a moment, and made a sudden gesture.

"I believe you. I may be a fool, but I know when a man tells me the truth. So I made a mistake, and you say he is dead; who are you, what are you doing here?"

"Trying to get out into the street unseen." Barnes smiled in his shy, whimsical manner.

"Ah, I knew he would fail!" she muttered, then collected herself. "Yes, yes, you are right not to trust me. We can trust no one. That is our punishment for thefts, lies, seductions, murders. And it is called patriotism—bah! Well, I knew Sheldon; he was a good friend. Now I must go to London. And you? Where do you go?"

"To London also," Barnes repeated. "I hope to hire a plane."

Her eyes narrowed, then she broke into a quick smile. "I see! Then you are completing Sheldon's errand! Good; we shall go to London together. Aren't you afraid I might try to rob you?"

"Yes."

So lovely, so charming was her smile, that Barnes was astonished once more.

"Oh, I like you! Suspect everyone, eh? Sheldon would have told you that. He told me he expected to meet someone here. Well," and she turned quickly aside, to show a small automatic pistol in her hand, "if I wished to rob you, I could do so. Come along! Let's get out of here before I get knifed in the back! That's Borescu's specialty."

"What's that?" Barnes started slightly. His eyes hardened. "His specialty! It was a knife in the back, thrown from the open window, that killed poor Sheldon! If I thought the murderer— but no. I can't remain here, or delay."

She laid her hand on his arm, looked steadily into his face.

"My friend, I know men; that's my business. I believe you, I like you. What you have just said, proves that Borescu must be here somewhere. Well, I am afraid; I confess it. Certain people have sworn to kill me, and here in this place I'm out of my depth. Give me three minutes, and we'll leave together. Agreed?"

Barnes nodded, and lit a fresh cigarette.

Without more ado, she set to work throwing her things into a bag; the art of light travel was clearly an old story to her. A curtain across one corner of the room provided a closet. She stepped behind this curtain, and he caught a flash of her bare arms above it. She was changing her clothes there.

Barnes looked away. Something at the window caught his eye, a moving object outside and clearly visible through the lace coverings of the sash. A hand and arm, moving across from beside the window, clutching at the knob of the sash and trying to open it.

Then the arm was drawn back. The window had opened a trifle.

Barnes quietly went to the window. Someone was outside on the balcony, waiting and listening. He got behind the slightly opened sash and waited. Miss Nicolas was humming a soft, gay tune.

She had come out from behind the curtain, and was closing her bag.

The hand appeared again. The window-sash was pushed inward. The figure of a man came swiftly into sight; a small man, crouched there, balanced, peering forward into the room. His arm swung up, and a knife was in his hand.

Barnes slammed the sash full against him, all his weight upon it.

THERE WAS a crash and tinkle of broken glass, a wild exclamation. The assassin was hurled back against the ancient iron railing of the balcony. It broke under his weight. From the courtyard echoed up a frantic scream, that ceased abruptly.

Barnes found the girl at his side, staring at the broken window, the empty balcony.

"It was he, Borescu!" she breathed. "I saw his face as he fell—"

"Get going," snapped Barnes. "Hear those shouts? It's my one chance to get out, while everyone's around his body. Step on it, girl! I hope the murdering devil is done for!"

He darted to the door. She caught her bag up and joined him; the stairs lay before them, empty. They hurried down together.

A moment later they reached the first floor landing. The stairs were still empty. But below, in the narrow hallway that served as entrance, stood two agents of police. Barnes knew that they were stopping all egress from the hotel. At this instant a burst of frantic voices from the courtyard alarmed the two agents; they swung around, broke into a run, and disappeared. Evidently the body of Borescu was causing a terrific commotion on all sides.

Next moment, Barnes stepped out into the street, holding the girl's bag. She took his arm, very calmly.

"The death of that assassin will make you a hero, my friend."

"Forget it," Barnes broke in curtly. He motioned to a taxicab that swerved in to the curb. "We're well out of a bad mess. Now, I'm going to put you into this cab. You go to Le Bourget, and if I don't show up in half an hour, play your own game."

"What?" Dismay rose in her eyes. "Do we not go together?"

"Not much."

The girl turned to him swiftly. "I don't know your name, but I owe you much," she said earnestly. "Believe me, I shall not forget. I understand; you wish to part with me now, and perhaps you are right. But in London, if you need aid, telephone Charing Cross three eleven and ask for Nicolas. I always pay my debts. Good-bye, my friend!"

And, to the utter astonishment of Barnes, she flung her arms about him and kissed him twice on the lips. Then she caught the bag from his hand and was gone into the cab.

"Le Bourget!" came her voice. "Quickly!"

The chauffeur grinned delightedly at the staring, dumfounded Barnes, and the taxicab went whirring away.

"Whew! What a flame of a girl she is!" thought the American. He signaled another cab. "Going by air, is she? Well, she's welcome. It occurs to me that, with so darned much dirty work going on, this airport is the one place in Paris that's liable to be unhealthy. That's where poor Sheldon slipped up. He came by air, and they knew it, and this knife artist was waiting for him."

He stepped into his cab, ordering the driver to the Hotel Terminus.

With this grim sequence of events at the Hotel Dupont, Barnes had abruptly changed his entire course of campaign. Air was the quickest system of transport, but for this very reason was also the most dangerous. Let the Nicolas girl go by air if she were fool enough to do so! Not he.

Barnes wanted to reach London alive. And dinned into his brain was the determination to accomplish his mission—at all costs.

His taxicab drew up before the dingy old pile of the Hotel Terminus, that once famous but of late rather notorious hostelry beside the Gare St. Lazare. Barnes left the cab, went straight into the hotel, and at the desk he secured a twenty-franc room, for which he paid in advance. He filled out the police registry slip in his proper name, displayed his passport, and was then shown to his room. He explained that his luggage would arrive later.

After five minutes he left his room and descended to the café.

Here he secured a sidewalk table and ordered a sandwich. It was twelve forty. At one ten, as he knew, a train left for Havre, an express that would reach there before dinner time. The question now in the mind of Barnes was whether he had thrown off any possible trailers. Even if not, he still had another string to his bow.

That evening the regular English line left Havre for Southampton, which it reached early in the morning. Altogether the slowest, safest and most comfortable route between Paris and London. Nobody in a hurry would dream of taking it.

At the next table, he observed a jovial fat man who had an expansive gold-toothed smile and a half bald pate. This gentleman settled himself with an aperitif and a copy of *L'Echo de*

Paris, and absorbed himself in the news. Barnes idly read the side of the folded paper that was toward him. But he watched the time as well.

One o'clock precisely. Barnes rose, flung down a note to pay the waiter, and then passed into the hotel by the front entrance.

He passed out at the side entrance immediately after. Heading straight into the station, he bought his Havre ticket, passed the gates, and lingered on the train platform to buy newspapers and magazines from the pushcart there. Preliminary toots of the engine, the calls and whistles of the guards, rang out. The train began to move. Barnes hopped aboard.

There was no crowd. Barnes presently found a first-class compartment that was empty, and esconced himself in it comfortably. He lit a cigarette, opened a newspaper, and patted the breast pocket in which the brown envelope reposed. Then he suddenly dropped the newspaper and reached into his pocket.

The brown envelope was not there. Gone!

CHAPTER III

BRIBERY

IN THE other breast pocket, Barnes found his passport and papers intact, of course. He thought back, swiftly.

True, that brown envelope had been a trifle large for his pocket; but who could have seen it? Who could have taken it? Certainly it had not dropped out. Suddenly he recollected how Miss Nicolas had flung her arms about his neck and kissed him with warm gratitude. At this, his eyes twinkled.

The smart little skirt! She had pulled the job off neatly. At thought of those impulsive kisses, and her quick getaway, his lips twitched amusedly.

"Much good it may do her!" he reflected. "If she did put one over on me, she hasn't gained much by her agility. And to think of her handing me all that line of talk, then calmly picking my pocket! So she's working for Italy, eh? Looks as though Sheldon had told her too much, friend or no friend."

The information that he carried was obviously of interest in more than one quarter. Everybody in the business was out to hijack him, apparently, and there were no rules in the game, as he had been warned. He had just saved the Nicolas girl's life, and she turned around and picked his pocket.

The guard came through, verified the first-class ticket of Barnes, and punched it. Five minutes later, a figure darkened the compartment door, opened it, and entered.

"With your permission, *m'sieu?* Thank you."

Barnes nodded. Then he took a second look at the man who settled down on the opposite seat—a look of incredulity, of startled recognition. Here was the fat man of the Hotel Terminus café!

The other met his look and smiled, showing the gold teeth.

"We have met before—ah, I remember! *M'sieu* was at the next table in the café, of course!" the fat man said cordially. "*M'sieu* is an American, yes? One observes the shoes, naturally. And the first-class travel. Me, I slip in after the guard has gone through, and it costs me nothing. But perhaps *m'sieu* does not speak French?"

Barnes shrugged. From the very slight accent, he took the man to be a German.

"Afraid I don't understand you, mister," he returned with a nasal drawl. "Don't mind me. I'll take a nap as we ride."

With this he pulled his hat over his eyes, laid back his head, and to all appearance dropped off to sleep. It was no trick to open his lids very slightly—enough to let him look down his nose at the fat, half-bald man opposite.

Barnes was by no means certain whether this might not be a mere coincidence. The fat man sighed, laid aside his hat, and mopped his shining dome. Then he took from his pocket a newspaper, folded in the French fashion, and began to peruse it attentively. The newspaper was the same *Echo* he had been reading at the café table.

It was folded in exactly the same way, he was reading precisely the same story, now as then.

That settled his doubts. And after a little he observed that the fat man, while pretending to read, was in reality furtively studying him.

Presently a man came past in the corridor. The fat gentleman glanced up, and behind the folded newspaper his hand made a gesture. The man outside nodded and passed on. At this, Barnes concluded that things were threatening to grow uncomfortably warm. He opened his eyes, looked at the fat man, and smiled.

"Just how many of you are there aboard?" he asked in French.

Without the least astonishment, the fat man laid aside his newspaper.

"Ah! You Americans are brusque and to the point, eh?"

His broad features fairly radiated jovial good humor as he spoke. And suddenly Barnes perceived how fearfully dangerous such a man might be. With a nod, the other went on in fluent English:

"I am glad to find you frank; one can do business with such a person." The little eyes bored shrewdly into Barnes. "You are no fool, Mr. Barnes. You are a wise man, I see."

"Eh?" Barnes started. "How the devil do you know my name?"

The fat man burst into a hearty, roly-poly sort of laugh.

"Oh, that is a mere detail! When you arrived this morning from London, we received you, without ostentation, of course. We knew of your coming, my friend. In the little hotel, out of the little hotel again, with that charming young lady! You see, I am quite frank. Now, would it please you to talk business? You are an American, and you know the value of money."

Barnes lifted his brows slightly; this was frankness with a vengeance! So his very coming had been known from the start. "Undoubtedly, money has value," he agreed. This fellow must have the prevalent European notion that all Americans would sell their souls for money. "You, however, have the advantage of me."

"Ah, a thousand apologies! My name, Mr. Barnes, is Rothstern. Let us see, now. Would a hundred thousand francs interest you? I am naming my highest figure. I warn you."

A glitter came into the eye of Barnes. "A hundred thousand francs? It certainly would, if I could get hold of it. That all depends on how it could be earned."

"Very easily. I ask only a few moments to look over the papers Mr. Sheldon confided to you. No one will know; the hundred thousand francs is ready."

THE EYES of Barnes widened in very real astonishment for an instant—astonishment that any secret agent could be so obtuse, so blundering. Still, this was evidently the nature of Rothstern himself. Barnes shook his head gloomily.

"Just my cursed luck," he muttered. "No harm in letting you see the papers, if I had them. I discovered it not five minutes ago."

"Discovered what?"

"The envelope's gone," Barnes said, with a dejected air. "All those business memoranda are gone! The girl you mentioned— she kissed me when we parted. No one else could have taken the envelope. A hundred thousand francs lost!"

The little eyes bit into him like gimlets.

"Come, come! You think to fool old Rothstern with such a story? It is true that she kissed you goodby. But to tell me—"

Barnes angrily broke in upon him.

"You don't believe me? Wake up to yourself. Good heavens— a hundred thousand francs just to look over those business agreements Sheldon made? Why, it would be like finding money!" His voice was shrill, impetuous, dismayed. "And now the envelope's gone! If you doubt my word, look for yourself. I've no luggage, search me!" And Barnes began to tumble things out of his pocket. "It was a brown envelope, sealed with red wax. I haven't got it, I tell you; it's gone! She must have taken it."

The fat features became grimly intent and appraising. The vehemence of Barnes was impressive. His agitation, his intense chagrin, his boyish excitement, could scarcely be doubted. Rothstern nodded again.

"So! You tell me such a story and expect me to believe it? Well, it is true that you could not hide the envelope, unless you put it behind your seat-cushions there.

"The brown envelope; yes, that is the one. You will let me see in your pockets, my friend?"

Barnes threw out his hands. "Of course; frisk me if you like. I tell you she got it; and she was going to London by air, too!"

"She is not such a fool," grunted Rothstern. Evidently he had come to the conclusion that Barnes was very much of a fool. "Will you kindly stand up—"

Barnes leaped to his feet. He had been in doubt as to his own course, but now it was plain enough. Rothstern had swallowed the bait of the brown envelope, and so had the girl. What had threatened to become a tragedy aboard the Havre Express, was now turning into comedy or even farce.

So the American made not the least protest as Rothstern swiftly searched him. He seemed quite as anxious as the other man to find the envelope, and even turned out his shoes at the grumbling demand. He carried no papers except his passport and a few personal letters, and it was obviously impossible for him to have concealed that brown envelope anywhere, without the flimsiest search turning it up.

"There are still the seat-cushions," Rothstern said, desisting at last from the search. Barnes, who had put on his shoes again, swore heartily.

"Look all you please. I'm going to the diner for a bottle of beer. But see here! I've told you what became of the envelope and where it is. I should get something for that, at least."

"Swine head!" the other grunted in German, then grinned. "All right, that is true. Here is a hundred francs, my friend."

Barnes took the banknote and walked out.

Not for nothing had he played his cards so carefully. Now Rothstern knew him as a mercenary American more than willing to betray his trust for a few dollars. Others would learn of it. The character so craftily established might, at some future time, prove invaluable to him.

BARNES WAS still sitting in the diner, lingering over his bottle of beer when the train entered Rouen. Exclamations of astonishment came from the waiters when it became evident that the non-stop express was, for once, halting. They peered out of the windows, and so did Barnes.

For the merest moment, the train halted and then rolled on once more. A smile touched the lips of Barnes as he saw three figures hurriedly crossing the platform to the station—the fat shape of Rothstern, and two other men. Barnes raised his glass.

"To your health, my friend!" he murmured under his breath. "At least the first round goes to the despised American amateur. And the first, let us hope, will be the last so far as you're concerned. You're at liberty to trail the girl, who can take care of herself and give you a headache to boot."

Presently he returned to his compartment, and for the remainder of the journey perused his magazines and newspapers undisturbed. That is to say, from without. As the train was nearing Havre, a very serious disturbance arose in his brain.

He was turning the pages of an illustrated French weekly, when the face of Miss Nicolas suddenly looked out at him. No doubt about it—the same! But it was the line of text below her picture that widened his eyes: "Mlle. Marie Nicolas, fiancée of the Grand Duke Alexis."

Alexis! That rascally old roué of a Russian exile, notorious all over the world for his rascality—about to marry this girl! The thing was preposterous.

"Still, it's none of my business," and Barnes shrugged.

"Damned shame, though. That sprig of nobility has been in more scandals and dirty messes than most, which is saying a lot. Well, better forget about it. Maybe it's not true. Even if it is, it's nothing to me."

So he dismissed the matter, a little scornfully, as one does when any charming member of the opposite sex becomes involved in the wrong way.

When the train pulled into Havre, he found himself with time to burn; the boat for Southampton would not leave until nine that night. He strolled about the old streets of the port section, and came at length to the long quays where the English boat and the little ferries for Deauville and Trouville lay berthed by the sheds of the customs inspectors. He stopped in at a nearby café and dined at his ease.

Later he sauntered on to the Southampton boat-shed. Taking nothing for granted now, he stood about smoking and narrowly watching the few people in sight. Freight was being sent aboard, and a number of cars returning from Continental trips. Barnes half expected to catch sight of the huge Rothstern again. Nothing would have astonished him by this time.

However, his critical eye discerned nobody who was in the least way suspicious. He purchased his ticket at last. With some jests upon his lack of any baggage, he passed through the customs shed and went up the gangplank. His passport had been looked over and returned without question, which argued that the Paris police might be looking for Smithson, but were not looking for John Barnes.

A steward led him to the cabin which he had engaged for his exclusive use. It was one of the de luxe cabins on the upper deck. He paused before it, as the steward unlocked the door and switched on the lights. Then he was aware of a voice coming from the adjoining cabin.

"No, no!" It was a low, tense voice, which brought Barnes around like a shot. The window of this next cabin, almost at his elbow, was a trifle open. "No, no! I tell you it is impossible! It would be murder!"

It was the voice of Miss Nicolas.

CHAPTER IV

MARIE'S TREACHERY

BARNES QUIETLY tipped his steward and dismissed the man. Then he switched off his cabin lights and stepped outside again. His feet made no sound on the resilient decking. Hereabouts all was deserted; few of these more expensive cabins were used, unless there happened to be a crowd aboard.

Barnes stood poised, waiting, outside that adjoining cabin window. That girl here—why, it was incredible! Or was it? Now he recalled what Rothstern had said about her going by air to London—"she would be no such fool." But how the devil could she have reached Havre, when she had not come on the express? By air, of course; or even by auto. She had let him think she was going to Le Bourget. Perhaps she, too, had figured this slower channel crossing as the safest.

In this, however, she had been far wrong. Barnes listened, then caught his breath. The man's voice that he heard was cold, suave, deadly. An English voice, assuredly.

"Don't try to charm me, you little fool; and they said you were smart! You flew to Deauville to lose yourself in the casino crowds, you caught the ferry over here, slipped aboard—and here I am. And do you know why? Because Rothstern was too cursed clever for you. He telephoned me to look out for you here. Come along; we know you have it. Turn it over or I'll squeeze your pretty little throat still tighter. I'd like to squeeze the life out of you as well! Damn you!"

There was an incoherent, strangling sound, a cough.

"I—I haven't got it!" the girl's voice gasped.

"You lie. We know all about it. You took it from him when you kissed him good-bye."

Barnes turned, and rapped sharply at the door of the cabin. There was an instant of startled silence. Then the man's voice made response.

"Who is it? What do you want?"

"Beg pardon, sir; it's the steward." Barnes made no effort to disguise his voice. He knew the girl was sharp enough to recognize it. "Shall I close your window, sir?"

A suppressed oath. "No! Go away!"

"Very good, sir."

Barnes tried the cabin door. It proved to be locked.

"Confound you, I told you to clear out!"

At this moment a shadow drifted across the deck. It became a man, who closed in upon Barnes and touched his arm, and spoke quietly.

"Here's half a crown for you, steward. You'd best get below decks and leave off bothering passengers who want nothing."

"Oh, thank you very much, sir!"

In the dim radiance reflected from the lights on the quay, Barnes made out a man of about his own height. So there were two of them! He took the proffered coin and turned away. Then he pivoted sharply, abruptly, and his left slammed home in a brutally low body-blow.

There was a gasping groan; the shadowy figure collapsed like a punctured balloon.

Barnes stooped swiftly. He caught hold of the limp figure, dragged it into his own cabin doorway, then inside, and stepped out again. He closed and locked the door. As he did so, the door of the adjoining cabin was flung violently open.

"What's going on out here?" It was the man's voice. "Stacey! Where are you?"

Barnes laughed softly, and stepped into the shaft of light, and down it full into the doorway.

"I'm afraid Stacey has gone on a long journey," he said lightly, whimsically. "At least, the police seem very glad to have hold of him."

HE PRODUCED a cigarette and lit it, but his eyes missed nothing. This staring man was tall, bony-featured, wide of shoulder. The face was powerful, lean-jawed, ugly. At the back of the cabin, one arm flung out against the upper berth, stood Miss Nicolas. Her hair and dress were disordered; one hand was at her throat, her wide eyes were upon Barnes.

"Who the devil are you?" snapped the Englishman.

Barnes waved his cigarette airily.

"A competitor, my friend, a competitor. Now, Miss Nicolas, hand over the brown envelope, if you please. You know me. My men are below and on the quay. The envelope you took from the American—quickly! Otherwise, you go to jail and this gentleman will follow his friend Stacey. At once, if you please!"

The crisp authority of Barnes' voice, his air of easy assurance, and the disappearance of Stacey, all seemed to cause the dark Englishman inexpressible alarm. He took a step backward, one hand flitting toward his armpit. Barnes merely regarded him with a smile, and the hand dropped. This man was dealing with the unknown; he was beaten.

"My friend," Barnes said pleasantly to him, with a glance at his wrist-watch, "you have exactly five minutes to get off the ship and the quay. As you know, it is a contravention of the French law to carry weapons. Get out, and do it fast. Now, Miss Nicolas, hand over the envelope."

The girl awoke. Her hand went to her bosom; she produced the envelope, now folded and crumpled.

With a subdued oath, the dark Englishman strode past Barnes, and was gone. Barnes swung the door shut. He took a quick step forward and caught the brown envelope from the girl's hand. He glanced at it, then gave her a quizzical look.

"Seals unbroken! Upon my word, you've wasted a lot of time," he said coolly. "And for a young lady so quick with her pistol where I was concerned, you were certainly meek enough when that rascal choked you."

She pointed to the floor. Her pistol lay there. Quick color rushed into her cheeks.

"You don't know him; Truxon is a devil!" she gasped out. "Oh, are you real? It can't be—it's impossible! How did you get here?"

Barnes perceived that she was close to hysterics.

"My dear Marie, you're scarcely the bold bad woman of fiction," he observed, with his warm and twinkling smile. "Upon my word, the more I see of you, the better I like you. Now, tell me why you took the envelope from me, in the first place. Second, why you didn't open it?"

The girl stooped, picked her pistol from the floor, and tossed it into the lower berth. She patted her hair into place, glanced at her torn dress. Barnes began to see that there must have been quite a struggle here before he happened on the scene.

"I owed Sheldon a good turn," she said, and looked him in the face with a hint of frowning wonder in her eyes. "I wanted to help him; and you seemed such a simpleton. You said you were going by air; only a fool would do that, when the air ports are so carefully watched. Why should I open it? I meant to deliver it—"

She broke off abruptly. The quiet smile of Barnes brought a flame of anger into her dark eyes.

"For whom are you working, Marie?"

"None of your business; so you don't believe me? Oh, what a fool you are—no, no." She checked herself abruptly. "No; it's you who made a fool out of me. You're clever; good lord, who'd have thought it of you? Walking in here like this! I owe you everything, yes; but you've made a fool out of me—"

"And you can't forgive it?" Barnes chuckled. "Calm down; keep your head. Nobody's a fool, I'm afraid. It's entirely due to me that Rothstern trapped you here. But who was this English-man who just walked out?"

"Truxon, of course."

"I honestly hate to corroborate your idea of my simpletonian quality—but who may Truxon be?"

"Still playing innocent, are you?" she said, with an air of scorn.

"If I weren't as innocent as a lamb, I might be in your shoes. You seem to be petrified with terror of everything around you. Borescu puts you in a sweat. This Truxon shows up and you bleat frantically—"

She became white with fury. Barnes paused, listening.

"I take it from the context that Truxon is working with friend Rothstern; yet he's apparently an Englishman. It's too complex for my simple brain. But am I correct in thinking that we're off at last?"

She nodded slightly, as though in relief. Excited voices were sounding faintly from the quay, winches had ceased rattling, and now the ship shuddered to the reverberation of her deep whistle.

"Tell me!" broke out the girl abruptly. "You must know that Truxon and Stacey were broken, smashed, fired out of the English service last year—and lucky they got no worse. But where is Stacey? I know he was watching while Truxon was in here. You had no men, no police—that was all bluff."

"Of course." Barnes started suddenly. "What the devil! I locked Stacey in my cabin. I'd better turn him loose and get rid of him—"

As he strode outside, he was thinking that after all he had learned everything he needed to know—except what he most wanted to know. The girl hesitated, then switched off her cabin lights and followed him.

BARNES FOUND his own cabin door ajar, the room empty. Stacey, obviously, had come to himself and escaped.

"The bird's flown—good!" he exclaimed.

Together in silence, they sauntered to the rail and stood watching the arc-lights of the quays float past and recede, the duller lights of the town blending in a mass and falling away, as the ship pointed out for the Seine estuary. Then Barnes was aware of her quiet voice beside him. She was herself again, composed and poised.

"I can't figure you out. Are you really as new in this work as you appear?"

"You flatter me." Barnes laughed a little. "Question for question. Are you really going to marry the Grand Duke Alexis?

She gave no evidence of surprise at the question.

"Certainly not. He thought I was, of course; on his part, he was merely after my money. It was all part of the Bulgarian affair, which is quite off the boards by now. But you haven't answered my question."

"My own question ought to answer it. I wish that I knew more about you. Then you are Bulgarian?"

"Heavens, no!" She broke into a short, amused laugh. "I'm an American, silly! Because my father had various electrical concessions over here I began to handle some deals for him, then I gradually worked into the game. It's not a nice game, at times, but I've made a place for myself. I just came from Rome. They made me a very flattering offer there, and it really tempted me."

"Tell me the truth," Barnes urged her quietly. "For whom are you working?"

"You wouldn't know the truth when you heard it," she said bitterly. "At the moment I'm working for no one, and tonight I'm a very humble and defeated person."

Barnes shrugged lightly in the darkness. So she would not come through and be frank! Yet the story that she told had fascinating possibilities; he almost believed it. He found himself liking her strangely, perilously. He liked her very weakness in the face of danger; too efficient a woman loses her most enchanting heritage.

"Yes, I'm new to the business," he said musingly. "So new, that I didn't even take it very seriously, I'm afraid, until—well, poor Sheldon's murder jerked me awake. Well, that's past; it's all over now. We're off for England, and all's well."

"You're optimistic," she said ironically. "You're taking up this business seriously?"

"I hope so."

"For whom, then? Who pays you?"

After information, was she? He laughed to himself. She would not believe the truth.

"Nobody. If some of us put ourselves, our money, our ability, at the service of our country, can anything in the way of money pay us?"

"I know; that's what Sheldon said," she replied in a low voice, to his astonishment. "Oh, I do wish you'd been in it before now! There are so many unsettled things a man like you should have handled, that were frightfully messed up by our diplomatists! Let's hope the new deal extends far and lasts long. Well, I wonder where Rothstern is now?"

"Probably in Paris, gnashing his teeth."

She laughed. "Not he! This business is a gamble; that's why I like it. There are no personalities; if you lose, take it like a sport and try again. But this Truxon is plain bad; so is Stacey. They're hired mercenaries, dishonored men, rascals, working today for the brownshirts, tomorrow for France. So you think we've left all trouble behind, eh?"

Barnes pointed back at the flashing lighthouse.

"There's the answer. Thank you for the 'we.' It's flattering."

"Your optimism is incorrigible. Well, comrade, goodnight and pleasant dreams!"

"Same to you. If you need me, call; I'm in the adjoining cabin."

He liked her firm, quick handshake. In fact, he warned himself frankly, he liked her altogether too much.

IN HIS own cabin, he found no traces of his late captive. How Stacey escaped from the locked cabin was a mystery, but it was significant.

"They're a tricky, fly lot, all this crowd of comic-opera assassins," Barnes reflected as he prepared for bed. "Keep one step ahead of 'em and you've got them cinched; that's the recipe. Hand 'em a new deal and they don't know what to make of it. So Marie didn't break into the envelope, eh? Just trying to help out a poor benighted countryman, eh? That's a good line, but I'd hate to trust her very far. Ten to one she's guessed that the brown envelope is a fake. Queer that Sheldon would do so much talking to her; he wasn't the kind to shoot off his mouth without a reason."

So pondering, he fell asleep with the envelope under his pillow.

An insistent hammering at his door finally aroused him to sunlight and the voice of a steward. The boat was docked, everyone was being turned out; and as he had left no call for breakfast, Barnes was just out of luck on this head.

He examined his effects; everything was intact, and there had evidently been no intruders. Dressing hurriedly, Barnes stepped outside and knocked at the adjoining door. No answer. He tried the door and flung it wide open. To his astonishment there was no indication of occupancy; even the berths were made up. Yet the girl had been in this cabin. Seeing the steward pass, Barnes summoned him. To his inquiry, the steward gave him a blank look.

"No, sir, that cabin was not occupied. You had the only one on this deck, sir."

"What? When you brought me up here last night, people were talking in there!"

"Yes, sir, a gentleman did have the cabin engaged, but he went ashore again before we left Havre."

Barnes made his way to the reception sheds. Who had lied to him, and why? He had certainly accompanied her to that cabin after their stroll on deck. Had Truxon engaged it, then? Perhaps; she might have had an entirely different cabin, and had said nothing about it. Yes, she had a shrewd little head and no mistake. Trusted nobody. She was as sharp as a whip—and what a good liar! Besides, he reflected, a fat tip to the steward would have caused that individual to lie fast and hard about the cabin being unoccupied.

The customs and passport formalities were quickly settled. Finding that he had ten minutes to spare before the boat-train departed for London, Barnes dashed into the refreshment counter for a bite to eat.

He was gulping his coffee down when there came a quick, lithe step behind him. He sensed her presence and swung around. Yes, she was there at his elbow, her eyes glinting with dark lights of danger.

"You! Well, I thought you'd skipped out!"

"You would think so," she said in a low voice, not without its touch of scorn. Despite everything, then, she still thought him something of a simpleton.

"I'm in debt to you, and I pay my debts," she went on under her breath. "Truxon went ashore at Havre. He flew across ahead of us. Now there's a small army of the worst rascals in Europe out to get you. Half a dozen of them are planted on the boat-train. They'll stop at nothing, and you'll never reach London alive."

"Whew!" Barnes whistled softly. "Looks as though we needed the good old interference play, eh?"

"Come along with me," she said, not asking him, but as though giving him the order. "I have a car and a chauffeur waiting. Hurry! We can drive up to London before the train gets there, and they'll not suspect. Come on."

She turned and was gone, giving him no chance to argue or question. Barnes followed her swiftly. In a flash he perceived that she had pitched upon the one chance to get through without trouble. He caught up with her at the station entrance.

"What about an appeal to the police?"

The question was rather inane and he knew it. She merely gave him one disdainful look, and went on to where a Daimler was drawn up. A chauffeur in whipcord held open the door. She entered; Barnes followed her in. The door slammed. The chauffeur slipped under the wheel on the right side, and next minute the car thrummed away and shot out like an arrow.

"By all means, this beats the train!" exclaimed Barnes, as they flashed through the streets of Southampton at top speed. To his astonishment, she flung him a look of sheer anger.

"You'd fall for anything, wouldn't you?" she snapped. "And I thought you were smart in spite of appearances!"

Barnes, mystified, blinked at her. Then sudden comprehension rushed upon him. Had she trapped him, after all?

He had no time to think, to speak. Even as he realized what must have happened, how easily he must have walked into her trap, the brakes squealed. The car turned a corner, ground to a halt, and a man from the curb leaped on the running-board. Next instant he was in the car, as it went on again. Barnes looked into a pistol.

"Keep your hands on your knees," snapped the stranger. "Sure he's the right one, Marie?"

"Yes," she said calmly.

CHAPTER V

CAUGHT!

BARNES LOOKED at the man, who occupied the jump-seat facing him and the girl. The stranger was dark, grave, intent; he meant business. Barnes turned to Miss Nicolas.

"I congratulate you," he said coolly. "I rather fancied that your confidences of last night were—shall I say, a little too frank to be real?"

"You would," she rejoined cuttingly. The reiteration of this phrase got under the skin of Barnes, brought a flush to his cheeks; her scorn of him bit deeply.

"Was there any truth at all in your recent story about Truxon being here?"

"Yes," she said.

Silence fell. The car rushed on. They were out of the city now, following a surfaced but narrow road at tremendous speed. The chauffeur was expert. He avoided other vehicles in the swiftly-jerking, abrupt English fashion that always brought the heart of Barnes into his mouth; he could never get used to English driving.

"Well," and Barnes turned to the girl again, with the whimsical smile which seemed to anger her, "my eagerness in leaping to your aid would appear to have been wasted, eh?"

"You seem to have a lot to learn," she returned, level-eyed and coolly poised again.

"Undoubtedly. You don't seem overjoyed at the success of your strategem."

Color came into her cheeks. "I hoped you'd have too much sense to fall for it."

"You really are an excellent liar, you know."

"Call me an actress and be less insulting."

"Insulting? Not a bit of it. I think you're splendid!" Barnes said warmly. She bit her lip, and her dark eyes flamed at him.

"Will you hand over what you carry, Mr. Barnes? Or must we use other measures?"

Barnes shrugged. "I have no choice. You've got me."

With a sigh, he drew the brown envelope from his pocket and handed it to her. She seized it impatiently—and flung it through the open window of the car.

"Simpleton! There's nothing but blank paper in that envelope. No more trickery, if you please! Hand over the real message!"

Barnes broke into a laugh of such genuine amusement that it brought confusion to her features.

"So you didn't waste your time after all, Marie?" he exclaimed. "Blank paper, eh? But that blank paper held secret writing, my dear—"

"It did not," she exclaimed flatly. At this instant, as the Daimler roared along the twisting, narrow lane between the English hedgerows, the chauffeur uttered a sharp cry and slammed on his brakes. They were around a sharp curve, and here the road was blocked. Two cars had halted, the drivers were talking together. The horn of the Daimler blared at them.

"Look out!" cried the girl suddenly. "Look out—"

Her partner, on the jump-seat, flung open the door and leaped out. There was a shot, and he staggered, then fell forward on his face. Several men had appeared from the hedge on either side of the road. They ran at the Daimler, pistols in their hands. The girl made an impulsive movement to rise, but Barnes swept her back with his arm.

"Quiet," he said calmly. "There's Truxon. Keep your head."

Truxon, indeed, coming forward to the side of the Daimler, while another man held the chauffeur covered and helpless. Truxon; lean, dark, savage of face, and there at the roadside was the man Stacey. The girl murmured his name. Barnes looked out at him with interest. A rather weak, vicious sort of face; this fellow Stacey had none of his friend Truxon's vigorous be-damned-to-you hardness.

"Good morning to you," said Truxon, unsmiling, lean, narrow-eyed, looking in at the two of them over his pistol. "Will you step along with me, or must I use force?"

"Just a minute," interposed Barnes. "I'm rather anxious to get up to London. If money will talk—"

"Nothing will talk except what I'm after—and you know what that is," Truxon said, meeting his gaze inflexibly. "Which of you has it, I don't know; you'll both come along. Yes or no?"

BARNES GLANCED at Miss Nicolas. She was white, her eyes desperate; obviously, this man Truxon inspired her with actual terror. She nodded and rose. Barnes followed her out of the car. Truxon, with a word of direction, piloted them over to one of the two waiting cars and got in with them. He told the man under the wheel to wait, and sat there with his pistol covering Barnes.

The other men flung themselves on the Daimler, beginning a minute search of the car. The partner of Miss Nicolas was lifted and placed inside; whether he were dead or wounded, Barnes could not tell.

A warning cry arose. Another car was coming along the road from Southampton. Truxon flung a command at Stacey, who walked back along the road and met it when it stopped. After a moment Stacey came along to the car in which the three sat, and was holding the brown envelope. He handed it to Truxon, with a grin.

"This was thrown out of their car a few miles back," he said.

"All right. Come along with us. Tell them, if they find nothing, to separate and let the Daimler go. That fellow is only shot in the leg. They can tie him up a bit."

Stacey fulfilled his errand, came back, and got in with them. Truxon flung an order at the driver, and the car moved off.

Barnes took the hand of the girl beside him, and patted it.

"Cheer up, Marie; you made a good try for it—"

"Shut up!" snapped Truxon. "Talk when you're asked, not until, unless you want a crack over the head."

Barnes nodded and kept quiet. He began to understand the paralysis of the girl before this man, whose lean, hard savagery held something inhuman. None the less, after a moment, he ventured to speak again, this time directly to Truxon.

"I'm apparently the person you want. You have me. Is it necessary to bother this young lady?"

Truxon grinned at him. "And let her go with the message, eh? Don't come anything like that. Either one or the other of you has it; and I'll get it. Now shut up."

The car swerved abruptly out of the surfaced road and turned into a lane. This ended at a pleasant old house, green trees about it, a low wall encircling the whole place. The gates stood wide ajar. The car swept in and halted directly before the house door. Truxon got out.

"Come along," he said, waiting, his pistol ready.

Barnes alighted, gave Miss Nicolas his hand, and caught a pressure from her fingers as she followed. Stacey came last. All four went into the house. The driver of the car left it where it was, and went around to the back of the house.

Truxon led his guests into a reception room, where an iron-jawed, elderly woman stood waiting. He nodded to her.

"All right, Wiggins; stand by. You two, sit down."

He tore at the brown envelope and brought to light a wad of blank paper sheets. He glanced at them, and handed them to Stacey.

"As I thought, a ruse. Just to make sure, have them tested at once for any secret writing. Marie, hand over that little pistol you don't know how to use. Quickly!"

The girl fumbled in her hand-bag. Wiggins, the hard-faced woman, came to her and caught the pistol out of her hand. Truxon nodded.

"Take her along, Wiggins, and go over her. Lock her in the east bedroom until I'm ready to talk with her. Report to me as soon as you've searched her. Run along, Marie; no protests, or I'll send Stacey to lend a hand with the search."

Stacey grinned at this. The girl flashed him a glance of contempt, then without a word accompanied Wiggins out of the room. Truxon turned to Barnes.

"All right. Will you hand over the paper we want, or not?"

"Paper?" repeated Barnes, with a puzzled air. "My dear fellow, that envelope was the only thing I have in the way of papers, upon my word! Surely you'll believe me?"

"Absolutely," said Truxon, with his mirthless grin. He handed over his pistol to Stacey. "Your job is to watch him every minute. Don't bungle it. Evidently there was nothing in the car. I doubt if she'll have anything. He's our meat."

Truxon went over to the door, that opened into the hall, and closed it. He came back and looked at Barnes.

"All right. Strip."

BARNES OBEYED without any useless protest. Realizing the prominence of the wrist-watch if he were naked, he tossed it on top of his shirt, finished stripping, then retrieved his cigarette case and took out a cigarette. Truxon snatched it from his hand, split it open, found only tobacco, and, with a grunt, handed him a cigarette and a match from his own case. Barnes lit the cigarette with a mild word of thanks.

Truxon slit every cigarette in the case of Barnes, examined the case narrowly, then examined Barnes from hair to toe-nails. He worked rapidly and in silence, but with obvious efficiency, while Stacey lolled in a chair and held the pistol. Upon a couch nearby lay a long dressing-gown of silk, obviously made ready in advance. When he had finished with the person of Barnes, Truxon picked this up and gave it to him.

"Thanks," Barnes said as he got into the silken gown. "I must say that your foresight in all directions is admirable."

Truxon paid no attention, but fell upon the clothes at one side. Every garment was examined minutely. The shoes bore the brunt of this, their heels and soles being slit; satisfied that they held nothing, Truxon bade his prisoner put them on again, and went on with his search. There remained his money, including the roll of notes Sheldon had given him, and the articles from his pockets. These Truxon put on a table, and sat down to his job.

The passport covers were slit and inspected. The pen and pencil were opened up. The larger coins were tested for hollow cavities. The paper money was held to the light and scrutinized under a magnifying glass, note by note.

Barnes waited, smoking, in silence. The wrist-watch, he had already guessed from its being out of order, was merely a hollow bluff enclosing the message. He tried to keep his mind off it, lest Truxon catch the mental wave. His personal letters came next. Truxon glanced over these, then tossed them through the air to Stacey.

"Have these looked over with the blank paper. Under the postage stamps, remember. I don't think we'll find anything there, but neglect nothing."

Truxon picked up the wrist-watch. He looked it over, examined the strap with care, then pried off the back of the case. He pried off a second and inner back. Like many cheap European watches, this consisted of small round works contained in a square case. Over the works, Truxon held the magnifying glass, scrutinized them and then the lids and the whole watch with care.

Then, with a shake of the head, he snapped on the two back lids.

Barnes pressed out his cigarette in an ash tray. Nothing in the watch after all, then. No message. What the devil did it mean?

CHAPTER VI

ESCAPE?

THERE CAME a sharp rapping at the door. Truxon rose, betraying no disappointment, and waved his hand at the clothes and other things.

"Take whatever you want, except the clothes," he said to Barnes, carelessly. "You'll not need them for a bit."

Stacey chuckled evilly at these words. Truxon strode to the door and opened it to show Wiggins outside.

"Nothing, sir," she reported. "I've locked her in there, but of course she can break out by the windows and get to the front entrance-roof."

"It'll do for the present," Truxon said. "I'll attend to her after a bit."

Barnes was standing at the table, stuffing the money, passport and other things into his dressing-gown pockets. Suddenly he was conscious that Truxon, from the door, was eying him keenly. Oh, clever Truxon! Just in time, Barnes was aware of the trap. He picked up the wrist-watch, looked at it, tossed it aside, pocketed his cigarette case. Then, as an after-thought, he took up the watch and negligently stuffed it into a pocket with the money.

Truxon came over to him.

"Barnes, I'm going to have that message," he said with calm, impersonal detachment. "It is now on your person. The chief terms of any secret Jugo-Slav entente wouldn't require much space. Well, you can imagine the next stage. I trust you'll not make things unpleasant for us? Here's your chance to hand it over."

Barnes looked at him, wide-eyed.

"The next stage? Oh, come, come! Surely you don't hint at medieval methods?"

"If I must, I'll burn it out of you inch by inch," Truxon said quietly. "Yes or no?"

Barnes merely shrugged.

"Come along," Truxon ordered curtly. "Stacey, follow on. We'll leave him in safety while you go over those papers."

Barnes knew now that he was a lost man; Truxon meant those words to the letter. And, when he had again picked up his possessions, he did exactly what Truxon had meant him to do.

He naturally would make sure of whatever held the hidden message. Somehow, of course, the secret must lie concealed in that wrist-watch.

He followed Truxon out into the hall, with Stacey at his heels. A stairway went to the upper floor of the house. Truxon strode on past this staircase, flung open a door underneath it, and disclosed a corresponding stairs that led down into the cellar. He turned a light switch and started down.

"Come on," he ordered.

Barnes followed him. On the second step, the American caught his toe, stumbled, and to save himself from falling, put out a hand to the wall. From the corner of his eye, he saw Stacey directly behind him and above.

Now, in a split second, Barnes acted. He caught Stacey's pistol-wrist and jerked at the man with all his strength, bending low as he did so. Caught off guard, Stacey was instantly unbalanced. The pistol exploded, drawing a sharp, agonized cry from Truxon below; probably the bullet struck him. Then Barnes had literally pulled Stacey over his head and sent him hurtling down through space, to crash into Truxon's figure.

With one leap, Barnes was back, catching at the door. He swung it shut, found a bolt, and shot it. Then, gathering up the dressing-gown about his knees, he dashed for the open front door and that car that still stood outside.

He was out of the house now, under the entrance portico, jumping for the car. As he reached it, a sudden laugh of exultation broke from him. The ignition key was still in the lock!

There was a crash, a tinkle of bursting glass. Barnes swung open the car door and glanced back. He saw Miss Nicolas scrambling from a window to the portico roof just above, and at the same instant, a pistol exploded somewhere. The bullet whined past his head and pinged off the side of the car.

Barnes leaped in, turned the key, and started the engine. As it roared, another bullet burst the windshield in his very face. The engine roared, and he reached for the gearshift lever. The girl was hanging from the edge of the roof. She came down with a rush, dropped, was up again.

The car moved. Miss Nicolas, panting, came scrambling in beside him, slamming the car door, sinking down breathless. The car pointed out for the open gates. Another bullet came crashing through, and another—

Barnes fell over sideways. He knew that the girl's hand had

caught at the steering wheel, her other hand opening up the throttle. He slumped down, falling into darkness.

"Looks like—you win," he muttered, and then went to sleep.

WHEN BARNES opened his eyes and looked up, he blinked in astonishment.

He remembered everything very clearly, up to a certain point. But he could not credit his own eyes. For there, standing beside his bed and smiling down at him, was Marie Nicolas—and with her, the ambassador!

"Welcome back, Barnes," said the ambassador quietly. "Glad to hear you're not badly off after all. I must say you've accomplished something new to London—coming to an embassy in a dressing-gown! You know Miss Nicolas, I think?"

"Too well," said Barnes faintly.

"Well, man—the message?" The ambassador pulled up a chair. "Did you bring it through? Miss Nicolas is one of us. She thought she could handle things better than you could; she was going to bring you safe on from Southampton despite yourself. Where is it? Didn't Sheldon give you a wrist-watch for me?"

"Oh—that!" Barnes gulped hard. "My dressing-gown pocket—"

On a nearby chair lay the silk dressing-gown. The girl snatched it up. From its pockets she tumbled everything out on the bed. With a swift exclamation, the ambassador pounced upon the wrist-watch.

"Thank heaven!"

One of us! One of us! Barnes could only lie there, staring at Miss Nicolas, those words burning into him. One of us!

Drawing out a penknife, the ambassador pried the crystal from the watch. With the blade, he carefully broke off the two hands. He then lifted up the cardboard face inscribed with hours and minutes. This came clear; beneath were several thin slices of paper. He detached these, then sprang to his feet.

"Excuse me, please. I'll have these decoded instantly."

Barnes found himself alone with Miss Nicolas. She sank down on the edge of the bed and met his gaze, a little color rising in her cheeks.

"Oh, don't look at me like that!" she broke out. "I'm supposed to be in Italian pay; yes, I'm really one of you, as he said. I should have told you, perhaps; but I dared not. Sheldon knew; he warned me not to let a soul suspect the truth. I really do some work for Italy, you know. I'm an utter fool. I've made a mess of everything. And you—oh, how you tricked us all! You, with your innocence, your naïve cantrap, your pretended childishness; a Sphinx, that's what you are! A rascal!"

She laughed a little as she looked down at him, a hidden tenderness in her eyes. But Barnes blinked suddenly. His face changed. He came to one elbow.

"What an idea!" he exclaimed. "My dear Marie, you've done something—upon my word! No, no; never mind now. Later on, perhaps. The Sphinx! The Sphinx! Exactly the thing!"

And, forgetting her, forgetting all else, he stared up at the ceiling with a glow of eagerness lighting his face.

III

FREE-LANCE SPY

The Sphinx played the greatest game in the world, a game for life and death—his own included—against the shrewdest spies of Europe.

CHAPTER I

A NEW GAME

IN THE darkness of a room overlooking the courtyard of
the old Hotel des Anglais, in Nice, a slight sound broke the
early morning silence. A warning bell, so thin and silvery that
it might have been imagination. Day after day, night after night,
Marie Nicolas had been awaiting this sound.

She swiftly flung back the covers, threw herself out of bed,
and over her nightgown drew a padded bathrobe. In her hand
glowed a tiny flashlight. The faintly reflected radiance showed
a glimpse of her dark and lovely features, her wide, hurried eyes
ablaze with excitement. Then darkness closed down again.

A large Bible was on her dresser. She snapped it open; the
book, made solid with glue and cut out in the center, was a box.
From this she took a set of head-phones. The tiny finger of light
touched a mark on the wall paper. She inserted a plug, pushing
it into the paper; the round points, so different from those of
American plugs, shoved neatly home. In her ears leaped a voice.

"They are fools, these Americans. Smart Yankees! I'll show
you the truth, Truxon. I've taken care of them, all of them. I
know everything about them."

Excitement set her pulses hammering. She could visualize
the scene in that room, only two doors away from hers. The
speaker was Rothstern; fat, jovial, with gold teeth and a shining
bald spot. One of the cleverest secret agents of all Central
Europe. Who employed Rothstern? No one knew, positively.

He was identified with Germany, but he might be working

*The pursuing
car closed in.*

for the Nazi party, for Hitler personally, for Poland, now the
close ally of Germany, or for any other cause.

Truxon? Yes, she knew this lean, dark, savage man, this renegade Englishman who had been kicked out of the British
diplomatic ranks. It was Truxon's room yonder, his and Stacey's.
Another of the same sort was Stacey, but weak and vicious,
diabolically crafty.

Now she crouched closer, listening intently. The dictaphone
worked perfectly. She had been two weeks getting it in place,
since learning that Truxon always occupied this same room
when in the city.

"They're not fools," cracked out Truxon's hard, smashing
voice. "They're smart. The smartest of them is that fellow
Barnes."

Marie Nicolas thrilled to the name, to the grudging admiration of this enemy.

"Barnes will be dead within the week," and Rothstern laughed softly. "Let me explain two things to you; this American activity, and the general situation."

"Damn the situation," growled Truxon. "I work for whomever pays me."

"I pay you." Rothstern spoke with abrupt authority. "Listen. Certain Americans like Barnes are working for their government. Idealistic fools, who place themselves and their brains and money at the service of their country; they have no standing, they have no acknowledged connection with Washington.

"They are free-lances who prate of bringing a new deal into diplomacy, of fighting us here in Europe with our own weapons."

The scorn in his voice was acid.

"Barnes is one. He pretends to be a fool, but is smart enough; however, he is in my hand. There's Hutton in Vienna, Morlake in Berlin, McGibbons in Warsaw, Pratt in Moscow, Williams in London, Reilly in Paris; also, there are half a dozen less important ones who have no steady position. Every one of these men is under the most strict watch. So is this girl, Marie Nicolas."

"What?" ejaculated Truxon. "But she's working for Italy!"

Rothstern laughed, and at his jovial laugh, Marie Nicolas trembled.

"So you think; so others think. She is really one of these American amateurs, my friends. She is here, in this same hotel; she has been here for two weeks, ill with influenza, or so she pretends. She leaves her room only twice a day, to sit in the sun in the courtyard. Well, she is attended to. Now, here's your pay for the next month."

A rustle of paper as banknotes were counted out.

"You don't care to go into the general situation?" Rothstern asked, with a note of mockery.

"No!" shot out Truxon. "Perhaps we know it as well as you do. We're only interested in earning our money."

"You shall earn it, I assure you. I have met this Barnes and know him well; he is open to bribery if rightly handled. But he's not the fool he looks, as you've found to your cost. On next Friday he will be in Ostend; you'll be there ahead of him, and so shall I. My work is to trap him; yours is to kill him. Understood?"

"Gladly," and Truxon's voice held a savage note of hatred. "But how?"

"How? Once and for all," and Rothstern's voice shook with laughter at his own jest. Then he sobered. "Now listen carefully. Next Friday evening, Ostend is to witness a gala performance of Beethoven's Solemn Mass, with chorus and artists from Paris. The king will attend. From Paris come a number of diplomats to attend, among them the American ambassador, and also Grimaldi, the Italian ambassador.

"Barnes is going to meet the American ambassador and obtain the signed draft of the tentative Abyssinian treaty."

"Abyssinian treaty!" echoed Truxon. "Are you insane? The States make a treaty with Abyssinia? That's nonsense."

ROTHSTERN'S JOVIAL laugh boomed out. "Ah, you know so much, you care so little for information! Well, never mind. There is much more to the business than appears on the surface. The main thing is that this man Barnes must be killed."

"Leave it to me," said Truxon.

"I can't leave it entirely to you. I must obtain the treaty draft from him."

"Sounds like nonsense," growled the renegade. "Why doesn't the American ambassador put it on the cables?"

"He has done so. We do not desire to keep it from Washington; merely to know its terms; so we prefer to intercept the original draft which Barnes is to take to London for inclusion in the diplomatic pouch to Washington. You see, these people have learned that we have a friend planted in the Paris embassy. They have become cautious."

"Looks to me, Rothstern," Truxon stated coolly, "as though you're lying about the whole thing; or you're covering up the real truth. Well, no matter. It's none of our concern."

"You are right, it is not," said Rothstern with a touch of asperity. "Barnes is the most dangerous of these American fools. He must be removed for good and all—ah! Someone at the door."

Silence; incoherent sounds, a mutter of voices. The crouched girl strained against the dresser in the darkness, shivering, but not with cold. Fear was in her heart, and not for herself alone! Then the voice of Rothstern exploded violently.

"A message for me! Give it here. Ah, a telegram, eh! It is—it is—ten thousand devils!" His voice broke in a passionate oath. "Greetings to our pleasant conference; signed merely 'The Sphinx, U.S.A.' Is this a joke? Damn you, answer me!"

The Sphinx! A thrill ran through the crouching girl. Then she started violently and turned. Outside her door was a step. It paused there.

She moved like a flash. Snatching off the head-phones, she silently slapped them and the cord into their false Bible, and next instant was beside the bed. She poised there, holding her breath.

A low, soft rustle came from the door, then ceased. The step sounded again, moving away.

AFTER A moment she threw the pencil-beam of her tiny flashlight on the door, then to the floor below it. A folded paper lay there; apparently a bluish French telegraph form. She went to it, picked it up, and opened it. It was no telegram, but on the form was typed in English:

THE FRENCH POLICE ARE ARRESTING YOU TOMORROW. CATCH THE PARIS EXPRESS AT 5 A.M. LEAVE TRAIN AT LYON, HIRE A BLUE RE-

NAULT WHICH WILL BE WAITING ON EAST SIDE
OF PLATFORM WITH A "FOR HIRE" SIGN ON THE
RADIATOR. IT WILL TAKE YOU TO BRUSSELS.

The only signature at the bottom of this message was the red
figure of a Sphinx, stamped there with a rubber stamp. Beneath
the figure were the letters, "U.S.A."

The Sphinx! She, and she alone, knew whom that could
be—whom it must be!

Suddenly she turned, darted to the dresser, seized her head-
phones again, and listened. She caught Rothstern's voice. "I tell
you, the French police are working with me! In this affair, France
is with us—but not openly. Yes, come along to my room. I'll
get the things you need, and there'll be no trouble at the frontier."

A door slammed. Silence. The girl swiftly put away her
phones again. She flashed the tiny light on her wristwatch. Four
A.M. It would still be dark at five. If she were to catch that
express for Paris—

The French police working with Rothstern? What .was it all
about? She had no idea. But she had been ordered to wait here
for some message from Barnes. On her own responsibility she
had arranged this dictaphone, this communication with Truxon's room. This hotel was well known to her. For the past two
years she had been on the go all over Europe. And now something had happened, something big was coming up. War? No
telling. All Europe was a hotbed of intrigue, of rivalry; France
and Italy stood out against each other.

The Sphinx! Her brain rocked with indecision. She remembered that day when she had called Barnes a Sphinx, and how
his face had lighted up. Now he had sent an ironic message to
Rothstern, another message to her. Barnes! Yes, it must be
Barnes, it could be no one else. Why was he adopting this
nom-de-guerre? Why were the police about to arrest her? They
had nothing against her. Yet she could not doubt. Rothstern
knew everything about this little band of gallant Americans

who were pitting themselves against the secret agents of Europe. They would have no recourse if they failed. They had no connection with Washington.

A thousand questions rioted in her brain; she sat with eyes closed, trying to evoke some order out of the mental chaos. Gradually it came. She must reach Barnes with what she had heard, yes! She had something definite now. Rothstern knew everything. Not one of the unofficial American agents, these free-lances who risked everything for their country, was safe. Rothstern knew of them all. He boasted that he had her in his hand. Yes, it was he who intended to have her arrested. How did Barnes know of it? Again the questions rioted. Again she beat them down, crushed them back. Nothing mattered now except to follow the orders of the Sphinx. Barnes? Ah—

She broke off abruptly, rose, switched on the lights in her room, after closing the window and drawing the blinds. She looked around. If there were danger from the police, she could not take away her belongings. She must abandon everything, her luggage, her clothes, and take only what she could carry in her handbag. No one must see her leave; well, that could be managed!

The holes in the wall paper she carefully patched; this room might again come in handy. The head-phones she must throw away in the street. Clothes, personal effects—she swiftly made her choice among them. Queer, that Barnes should know what the French police intended! It was two months since she had seen him; in this interval he had completely dropped from sight.

Now she was clear-headed, cool, alert. She left money for her hotel bill, with a note asking to have her effects held; she had gone to Menton for a few days. This might throw the police off the track. If only she did not have to buy a ticket and a place in the train! There was the danger-point, if the police were on the lookout. Room lights off, she slipped out into the deserted corridor.

IN THE street, the chill wind of coming dawn, the sparse

lights, the emptiness and absence of life, appalled her. She came into the Boulevard Gambetta; a long way still to the station. A glance at her wrist-watch and she stepped out more briskly. Only twenty minutes left now.

With a hoot-hoot and a flicker of yellow, lights, a taxicab rattled along behind, overtook her, and passed on. She paused, shivering. From the open cab window, floated a laughing voice; the hearty, jovial tones of Fat Rothstern, accompanied by the harsh, inhuman laugh of Truxon. She faltered. On their way to that same train? No help for it. She feared Rothstern more than the renegade Englishman, because his merry deviltry was abnormal. The same train? Well, she must go on. She had her orders.

Resolute, she hastened on with something very like a suppressed oath at her own heart-hurried fears. After all, she could take care of herself. She was the equal of any man of them, as she had proved ere this. What folly, to let the chill morning darkness oppress her! A laugh, and she flung off the weight. The thrill of it all seized upon her. Her pulses leaped to the fervor, the quick chances of the game.

She took the short-cut out of the Place Franklin. Two bicycle police rolled along, eyed her sharply, went their way. Ahead opened the width of the Avenue Thiers and the railroad, the glittering lights of the station beyond. The train was there; the engine was huff-huffing like all French engines. No time to lose if she were to make the express!

Suddenly a man appeared ahead, a dark, thin man, a stranger. He was aiming to intercept her. Hand flew to bag; her little pistol was jerked out. She went straight at him. Then, to her astonishment, she heard her own name.

"Mademoiselle Nicolas, is it not? Correct. Your *billet*—everything. Hurry!"

She took the envelope thrust at her. The man turned away and was gone, slouching off into the shadows. Hurriedly, she examined the envelope. Yes; a seat to Paris, a ticket to Paris.

Also a ticket to Lyon. She understood in a flash. She must show the Paris ticket in case she were traced. At Lyon, where she would leave, she must give up her ticket before getting out of the station. No Frenchwoman would give up a Paris ticket before getting halfway there; hence, the Lyon ticket to avoid comment.

Who had done this? She caught her breath, as she turned over the envelope in her hand. Upon it was the rubber-stamp of the Sphinx. Barnes? No, no, that was impossible. Barnes knew his way around Europe, but he was an innocent, a new hand at this game. She must be on some false scent after all.

The whistles of the guards were shrilling when she came on to the platform. She had one glimpse of Truxon standing there, tall, lean, savage, waving his hand. Rothstern was on this same train, then!

CHAPTER II

DISGUISE

DAYLIGHT CREPT down from the Alps, with Toulon still well ahead. It would be afternoon before they reached Lyon. Sunlight filled the morning. Marie Nicolas wakened from her nap, stretched, found her handbag and little toilet case at her side, and her brain leaped alert instantly. She forced herself to forget all the mystery of the night, even the dark stranger who had supplied her with tickets. She now had to face the danger of the day, with Rothstern on the same train.

Fortunately, she was no longer an apprentice at this business. She had brought with her all she needed.

She went into the dressing room between the compartments, glanced into the next compartment and found it empty, and went to work rapidly. She grimaced into the mirror at her neat, trim face and figure, her warm cape and the Rue Vignon dress.

She was indeed very lovely, the essence of good taste; well, this must be altered!

Her masses of dark hair were rearranged in careless, sloppy fashion. Cheap, musky perfume was liberally splashed about her dress. She deliberately ripped her chic little hat and sewed it together again, a flimsy ruin; the lines of her dress, her figure, could not be spoiled, but the set of the dress could be spoiled with a reckless tug here, a pull there. When she looked in the mirror again, it was with a sigh.

Now for her face. Gaudy, splashy earrings were nipped in place, dangling almost to her shoulders. Deft touches darkened her brows, changed their contours. Darker skin about her eyes, the lids darkened; a hideous, flashy lipstick completely out of harmony with her complexion changed and spoiled her mouth. Last of all, glasses; pince-nez that really pinched. Another grimace when she inspected the result.

"A woman in the worst possible taste—can it be you?" she observed cheerfully. "Yes, it really is little Marie; but who would know it? Especially a man. And the hair, the hair! That's the best of all. Marie Nicolas, you're a perfectly horrid person—and hungry!"

All this had taken time. The dining-car messenger appeared, reserved her a place, and went on. She left her cape behind, bunched her dress still more shapelessly, and ventured forth.

She was early; she wanted to be early. The train was wakening as it thundered along. Tourists of all kinds, many French, but few Americans; the rate of exchange kept Americans out of France, these days. Fortunately, the restaurant car was close at hand, and with relief she entered and found herself placed at table. The waiter addressed her significantly in English; she, who was invariably taken for Russian or French, was now an obvious tripper! She smiled brightly.

Then, for an instant, she shrank, and her pulse stopped. A presence behind her, a jovial, hearty voice—Rothstern. Coming in with another man.

"Yes, *garçon*, yes, a good breakfast," she exclaimed in an abominably harsh voice. Her English accent made the waiter wince. "Muffins and everything. And don't forget the marmalade, my man. Right!"

To her horror, Rothstern paused at the next table. Then he turned his back; he sat down with his back to her. She could see the shiny bald spot, the clipped hair, the roll of fat above his collar—but thank heavens, he could not look at her! For an instant she closed her eyes, then opened them.

They dilated. Incredulity came into her face and passed. For there, sitting opposite Rothstern and chatting gaily with him, was Franklin. Young Franklin, the laughing Baltimore boy who was the latest recruit to the free-lances; he was supposed to be in Rome, getting on to the ropes. And Rothstern had him in tow!

She watched them. Once or twice Franklin's gaze rested upon her and flicked away again. He looked tired, a bit drawn, but evidently he was charmed with Rothstern. Most men were, who did not know him well. Marie could hear Franklin's voice at times.

"Yes, a bit of business in Paris. Importing is pretty well wrecked these days… sight-seeing in Italy. Wonderful place under the Facist régime! No, I didn't hear any talk of war… in the wine business, eh? You speak perfect English, really!"

From what snatches of talk she caught, the girl gathered that they occupied the same compartment. Was this by chance? She doubted it. Was it by chance that she was on this train with Franklin? The question startled her with its implications. How far ahead did this unknown Sphinx see and plan? Questions be hanged! She dared not let them engulf her, and resolutely put them aside.

Somehow she must warn the young fellow. That he did not recognize her was quite evident. It was unfair to pit him against the veteran Rothstern, who had already enmeshed the boy. As she lingered over her breakfast, more questions rushed upon her; what was going on, what game was being played out with its final scene reaching up to Ostend in Belgium? She could not guess. She struggled to keep her mind on the business in hand, on her own perilous strait.

Toulon was behind them; the train was creeping on westward to Marseilles, before it turned north to Avignon and Lyon. Suddenly the bulk of Rothstern heaved up. His voice came to her clearly.

"You will pardon me? I must prepare telegrams to go from Marseilles. We may meet again on the platform, eh?"

Telegrams, eh? The fat fox was up to something; yes, the boy must be warned. Rothstern brushed past the table of Marie Nicolas without a glance and went his way. Quickly, the girl seized pencil and a scrap of paper.

> *I am Marie Nicolas. Destroy this. The man with you is Roth-*
> *stern. He knows every one of us. If you bear any messages look out.*
> *Keep away from me.*

Presently Franklin rose, paid his bill, and started past Marie's table. Her handbag was knocked from the edge as he passed, though not by his doing. He halted, and with a word of apology stooped for it. As he rose and handed it to her, she slipped the note in his hand. He gave no sign of astonishment, but went on and was gone.

She breathed more easily. After a moment she, also, paid for her breakfast and departed. On the way back to her compartment she kept a sharp eye out, but saw nothing of either man; therefore, they must be beyond her car, toward the rear of the train.

THEY WERE flashing into Marseilles now. As by magic, the station appeared and the express slid to a smooth halt. Ten minutes here. Marie opened the door and stepped out to the platform. The news-wagon was almost opposite. She bought Paris editions of English papers, a couple of English magazines, and ducked back into her own compartment again. She had not seen a paper, except the French journals, for two weeks.

Minutes passed. Suddenly Franklin appeared, opening the compartment door that led into the passage. He came suddenly, his voice leaped at her.

"They've got me. Do your best—"

Something flashed in the air and fell at her feet. An envelope. She kicked it under the seat. Franklin was gone; at the same instant, the outer door was wrenched open and two Frenchmen entered, typical business men. Politely, with many apologies, they asked if they might share the apartment. She affected ignorance of French. One explained himself in halting English. Marie Nicolas shrugged, nodded, and opened up her newspapers. The two Frenchmen settled down, deep in talk.

Men moved rapidly past the passage door. After a moment, glancing out at the platform, she saw Franklin there with several suave gentlemen; he was being arrested, then. The engine whistled, the guards slammed the doors, the train moved out of the station. Arrested! Then Rothstern had done it. And her warning had come barely in time. That fat devil was checkmated for once, thank heaven!

The guard appeared, verified the first-class tickets of the two Frenchmen, and went on. Suddenly their words reached into her consciousness.

"Did you see the statement of Count de Prorok, the explorer? He has just left Abyssinia. He says the Italians have massed troops in their colony of Eritrea and are preparing to seize Abyssinia, that France and England have consented, that Italy has caused the frontier fighting. It means war!"

"Bah!" was the response. "No one knows or cares anything about Abyssinia. It is the Balkans that should worry us!"

"No worry," said the first. Marie abruptly realized that she was listening to a keen analyst who knew whereof he spoke. "England, France, Germany, want no war. Russia allied with the French, wants no war. Mussolini will keep the peace, depend on it! He'll permit no Balkan conflict. All this is a mask; he intends to seize Abyssinia. Forty years ago, an entire Italian army was destroyed there, at Adowa, and Il Duce means to avenge the loss and seize the whole country. Just as Prorok says. Another Manchuria, my friend!"

"Well, you should know." And the other laughed. "You have a nose in the Quai d'Orsay. But what is it to us, to France? Let Italy rule the black savages. Her rule will be good for them."

"Shall we step out into the passage and smoke?" was the reply. "This Englishwoman will be sure to object if we smoke here—"

The two left the compartment. Marie Nicolas leaned over, picked up the fallen envelope, and glanced at it. Sealed, and addressed only to John Barnes. She thrust it away beneath her dress and pinned it there securely.

She returned to her papers. There, she found the key to the conversation she had just heard; conflict on the borders of Abyssinia and Eritrea, an appeal to the League of Nations by the former, a refusal of any arbitration by Mussolini. So Il Duce would keep the peace in Europe in order to have a free hand in Abyssinia? Very likely. She shrugged and dismissed the matter as of no interest.

SUDDENLY, WITH a leap of the pulse, she remembered what Rothstern had told his two mercenaries. A commercial treaty with Abyssinia? It was nonsense, on the face of it. The United States had no commerce, no interests, there. Then why was Rothstern so desperately set on learning the terms of this alleged treaty?

"More questions," she muttered angrily. "Plague take them all!"

Back to the newspapers. A short, sharp exclamation broke from her; she stared at the news items with distended eyes. Morlake in Berlin, Hutton in Vienna, had been arrested the previous evening. American business men, charged with espionage. And both were members of the free-lances! Rothstern again, striking savagely. Why?

The two Frenchmen came back into the compartment, apologized politely, and went back to their rapid French conversation in supreme confidence that their fellow-traveler could not follow. The one who had his "nose in the Quai d'Orsay" explained a detail to his companion.

"I tell you, a month ago ships went out of Marseilles loaded with munitions for Abyssinia! There is only one railroad into that country; we control it. Are we letting arms reach the Ethiopian emperor? Then why this disregard of treaties? It looks singular. Watch. You will see things happen in that country."

A fat shape bulked against the glass of the passage door, looking in. Rothstern. Then he went on. A sense of suffocation oppressed Marie Nicolas. The Frenchmen had switched to a discussion of business conditions. She listened no longer.

The express rolled on to the north. The Sphinx, the Sphinx! Incredible as it seemed, this might be Barnes. At least, he had given Rothstern and the two renegades a startling surprise with his telegram. He seemed to be aware of their secrets; no, he could not be Barnes, after all. A glow crept into the girl's eyes as she thought of him. A splendid fellow, Barnes, but new at this business. No, he could not be this mysterious Sphinx.

Avignon fell behind; a brief stop only. Crossing the river, she had a glimpse of the storied castle of the Popes, with its towering height and the broken bridge below. No stop now until Lyon.

The chief of the train, the "conductor" in America, made his appearance, heavy with gold braid and authority, as befitted a trusted employee of the government. He beckoned the two Frenchmen outside and there, in the passage, conferred with them; many shrugs, gestures, explosive sounds. Finally they appeared to agree. A guard arrived and came in, taking their luggage out. They all vanished up the corridor.

Another guard came in sight, carrying two suitcases, an umbrella, a portable typewriter. He lugged them in, disposed of them in the racks. The girl spoke quickly.

"Is someone else coming in here?"

"But yes, *ma'mselle*," he responded, touching his cap. "A rearrangement, you comprehend; many passengers came on at Avignon. A gentleman from the second class is moving in here. It will not inconvenience you."

She could not reply. The words died in her throat. For there at the door was the gentleman from the second class. It was Rothstern.

He entered, tipped the guard, and lowered himself upon the opposite seat. He did not glance at the girl. His heavy, jovial features were intent upon a number of telegrams which he must have received at Avignon. At length he stuffed them into his pocket, picked up a newspaper, and began to peruse it.

Marie Nicolas sat reading. She felt stifled; her thoughts were inchoate; terror was upon her. She, who was supposed to be so fearless, so well able to take care of herself, stood in absolute fear of this man. She could face the brutality of Truxon, but the gold-toothed smile of Rothstern unnerved her.

She became aware of furtive glances stealing at her. What to do? She could not leave without making a scene, if he were really suspicious of her. If not, her best bet was to keep quiet. Suddenly he chuckled slightly and laid aside his paper.

"Madame is, no doubt, a tourist?" he said in English. The girl gave him a cold look through her glasses, and returned to her magazine.

"The eye is a wonderful organ," he went on, with another chuckle. "When it follows lines of type, it moves back and forth, one sees it at work. But the eyes of madame are fastened upon one point, they do not move—"

"Sir, are you determined to be insulting?" demanded the girl icily.

"A thousand pardons!" said Rothstern humbly, and spread out his hands. "I merely pass the time with observations. I am a philosopher."

He paused to light a cigarette. Marie Nicolas felt a cold, chill thrill pass up her spine. She knew what was coming; and she was right.

"Elimination," murmured Rothstern, as though to himself, "can solve many things. A young lady disappeared from her hotel at Nice. I learn of it later on. I determine that she must be on a certain train. I search, I see nothing of her. I speak with my friend the conductor. Yes, a young lady bound for Paris did come aboard. She is not the one I seek, obviously; yet I think she must be the same. One thing she cannot change, and that is the little foot. The shoe made in America is so obvious in France! So is the shoe made in England—but she does not wear the English shoe."

M A R I E N I C O L A S shrank for a moment, conscious that the blood had drained from her face. Then she quietly laid down her magazine and looked at Rothstern. He met her gaze, a twinkle in his eye, his jovial laugh showing his gold teeth.

"So?" he asked. "You would not tell a lie to old Papa Rothstern, *hein?*"

She knew the grim, ruthless cruelty behind that laugh. "Not much use trying to fool you, is it?" she said quietly.

"Not a bit. Ah, now you are sensible!" Rothstern beamed upon her. "Why did you run away from the hotel at Nice, my dear?"

"To see where you went, if you must know."

Rothstern chuckled. "Good. We are in company; we go to Paris together. Now, my dear Marie, shall we be frank and abandon all fencing? Good. Perhaps you caught this train to meet Mr. Franklin, *hein?* And somehow, somewhere, he gave you what I want very much to have. Perhaps you warned him, even, about poor old Papa Rothstern."

The girl shrugged. "Yes, I did. But I didn't know he was on the train until I saw both of you together. After that, I had no chance to speak with him again."

"Evasion, eh?" Rothstern rubbed his pudgy hands—big hands, massive hands they were. The gesture chilled her. "Very good. No doubt you have read the paper there. No doubt you saw what happened to poor Franklin; an estimable young man whom I had no chance to warn. Very well. Now, suppose we are friends, eh? Suppose you tell me something I want to know. We lunch together, we reach Paris friends, and part. I will protect you against anything unpleasant, such as happened to poor Franklin. You will not do badly to have Papa Rothstern for a friend, Miss Nicolas. Yes or no?"

"What do you want to know?" she demanded. The threat was clear enough. She would be arrested if she refused. Probably she would be arrested anyway, later.

"Just who is the gentleman who calls himself The Sphinx, U.S.A.?"

She started, her eyes widened. "But I can't tell you that! I must not tell—at any price!"

Rothstern beamed. "The price? It is simple. You remain free, my dear, as you should remain. Come; I see you know. Tell Papa Rothstern."

Beneath his joviality the threat began to appear more pronounced.

"If I tell you—but no, no, I cannot!" she exclaimed in agitation. "No one—"

Rothstern's ponderous features came closer, as she shrank. He seemed fully aware of the terrifying effect he exerted upon her.

"The French police can be most unkind to a poor prisoner," he suggested. "It would pay you, really, to make a friend of me. And nobody would know, upon my honor!"

"I—could—I trust you?" she breathed, staring wide-eyed. "But wait! I must send a telegram from Lyon.

"We shall lunch together, then. If when we leave Lyon I feel that you won't betray me—I'll tell you."

Rothstern beamed, and nodded. "Good! We shall have a nice luncheon with champagne, my dear. Ah, if I were twenty years younger! But we shall see. Yes, you'll find that it pays to trust Papa Rothstern."

She shivered a little, thinking of the envelope pinned within her dress.

CHAPTER III

PURSUIT AND SUBTERFUGE

JOHN BARNES stood on the station platform at Lyon and waited for the P.L.M. northbound express.

Over one ear was cocked a disreputable chauffeur's cap. Over the other ear, in the approved chauffeur's custom, was tucked a spare cigarette. A dirty white chauffeur's dust-coat, the French survival of a prehistoric motoring age, cloaked most of his body. He had a sandwich in one hand, a bottle of *vin blanc* in the other, and excitement blazing in both eyes.

A thin, dark man drifted up to the lunch-counter, bought a sandwich, and began to eat it. He drifted away, paused for an instant beside Barnes to inspect his sandwich suspiciously, and spoke under his breath.

"M. Franklin was taken off the train at Avignon by agents of the Sûreté. I just got the wire."

"Cover the exit gate," muttered Barnes, and the dark man drifted on.

You must see Barnes as he stood there, munching ravenously, drinking from the bottle, dirty hands, face ingrained with dirt and beard-rubble. An impudent chauffeur type, a humorous glitter in his excited eyes, a strong, hard jaw, lean in the sunlight as he tipped his head back to drink. And those stabbing, dancing gray eyes of his covered everything in sight. A man playing the greatest game in the world, and playing it for life or death. His own included.

Let us suppose, to get the picture, that a Frenchman stands

before the lunch-counter of the Pennsylvania station in Phila-delphia. The Federal secret service is after him. The local police are watching for him. The railroad detectives have his descrip-tion. And he stands there, eating, drinking, laughing, ready to pull off the biggest coup of his career! That was the situation of John Barnes as he waited.

The sandwich gone, he finished the bottle, handed it back over the counter, took the cigarette from behind his ear, and struck a match. At the other side of the platform a south-bound train had pulled up, and people were drifting everywhere. A French station platform is like a jail. To get in and out, one buys a ticket; to leave it from a train, one gives up the railroad ticket. Barnes took the ticket he had bought and held it ready in his hand. The north-bound express was coming in. He made his way toward the nearest exit, glanced at the guard there, then turned to watch.

There was the express now. News-wagons trundled out, wine and sandwich wagons; police strutted about importantly; porters rushed about, their straps aswing. Barnes puffed at his cigarette, motionless. The express came to its swift and silent stop. Bells clanged, whistles blew. Passengers began their frantic concourse, shrieking at porters. The carriages were emptied, everyone strolling up and down.

A girl appeared. Barnes threw away his cigarette, pulled down his cap over one eye, stood tensed. Marie Nicolas, holding a telegraph blank in her hand, hurrying. Behind her loomed up the fat figure of Rothstern, overtaking her with a jovial laugh. She swung around Rothstern took her by the arm.

Like a flash, she slapped him across the face, hard. Her voice shrilled up in a torrent of rapid French: "Dirty pig! You would insult a woman of France—oh, to me, to me, *messieurs!* This *sale cochon* of a German would insult me—"

Instantly, the platform was in an uproar. From all sides, Frenchmen came on the jump. Rothstern, incapable of a word, was surrounded and drowned in a rushing hostile mass of figures.

Barnes turned to the exit, gave up his ticket, and strode swiftly out to the street. There, where a blue Renault stood with a "For Rent" sign on the radiator, was a dark, sad man. Barnes made him one quick gesture, and got into the car. The other turned and departed at a run and was gone around the next corner.

Out from the exit slipped the figure of Marie Nicolas. One swift look, and she came toward the car. Barnes swung open the door. Without hesitation, she ducked in and slammed the door behind her as she half fell on the rear cushions, the car already in motion.

With a swoop and a roar, the Renault went leaping away.

"M'sieu," came the girl's voice from behind, breathless, excited. "Are you sure that it is all right? You expected me?"

"Hold your breath, baby," said Barnes in English, and chuckled. "Change cars at the next transfer stop. This is fast work; no time to talk."

A startled gasp from behind, and he chuckled again. Then he settled down to business.

He drove fast and hard for five minutes, dodging traffic and rounding corners like a madman. Then he slowed. A garage appeared ahead, before it a large gray roadster, and beside the roadster, the same thin, sad, man who had departed so hurriedly from the station. Barnes came to a halt behind the roadster, which bore an English license.

"All out, Marie!" he exclaimed, and ducked from the front seat. With a swift movement he was out of his cap and white robe. "Ready, Eremian?"

"Quite, monsieur." The thin, sad man handed him a little packet. "Passports, touring permit, everything. Here is the driver's license in your new name."

"Good. In with you, Marie."

HE SETTLED under the wheel of the roadster, Marie Nicolas beside him The car leaped away. Ten minutes later, they had passed the city tax-barrier without question. Then Barnes drew a long breath, and glanced at Marie, his gray eyes dancing merrily.

"Made it! By glory, that was a tight squeeze, young lady. Did you see Franklin?"

"Yes. He gave me a letter for you."

"Thank heaven! Keep it for the present. How are you?"

She gestured helplessly. "Bewildered. Utterly bewildered. John Barnes, you're not the same man I knew!"

A joyous, eager laugh escaped Barnes. "You bet I'm not! But I've got you safe away out of the smash."

"It looks crazy to me," she said. "I could have got across the border from Nice without heading north over the whole of France."

"Not a chance," Barnes said decisively. "Every road, every border station, on the south and east, was stopped this morning. This trip, we've got the whole of France against us. Germany as well. What I predicted to our ambassador in London, months ago, has happened. Every one of our men has either been clapped into jail or is under the closest sort of scrutiny; they've smashed our organization, Marie."

"And Rothstern did it. He said so," she cut in swiftly. Then she caught the arm of Barnes. "Tell me! Are you the Sphinx? Are you?"

Barnes gave her a quick, hard glance, then watched the road again.

"Yes. I thought you'd guess it. I heard of Rothstern's coup just one jump too late. He's tried to clear the slate at one crack, and he's darned near done it, too. Half Europe is behind him— just for this one occasion. Two weeks from now, the storm will be over; but right now we're sure in the soup all around."

"But why?" she demanded. "What is it about? Is there really an Abyssinia treaty?"

"Good Lord!" Barnes flung her a look of startled wonder. "How the devil did you catch on to that? You certainly are a marvel! Go on, talk. That was a lovely getaway you made on the platform. Tell me about it. About everything."

"For one thing, they plan to get you when you go to that musical thing at Ostend, to meet the ambassador from Paris. Truxon has that job."

Barnes started, then whistled softly. "Damn it! They have a spy in the Paris embassy; we can't locate him. All right, tell me how you know so much."

Laughing, she complied, delighted at having puzzled him, and still lost in wonder at finding him to be the Sphinx in sober earnest. And as she talked, Barnes kept the roadster roaring to the northward at high speed.

What a girl she was! Her vibrant personality, her keen ability, fascinated him. She was the one person he had determined to save at all costs, from this sudden debacle which had burst upon the little company of free-lances. She was worth all the rest; not because she was a woman, or from any personal interest, but because her wits, her brain, was worth the others combined.

"There you have everything," she concluded. "Is it really something about Abyssinia? What we could have to do with that country, I've no idea."

Barnes nodded frowningly. "We have. Their envoy in Paris has arranged terms with our ambassador there; tentative terms, to be confirmed in Washington. The mutually signed draft is the crux of this situation. It must go by special messenger, and getting it out of Europe is the very devil. Why, I'm not sure. Why Rothstern must have the terms, I don't know. Abyssinia no doubt hopes that a special treaty throwing her borders open to our commerce will forestall Italy, for Mussolini is intent upon grabbing the country. Reilly is to meet us at Dijon, if he gets out of Paris safely.

"He'll know the answer, and why France is so suddenly backing Rothstern's hand."

"But, tell me about yourself, about the Sphinx!" exclaimed the girl eagerly. "How did you send those messages to Nice? How did you have those tickets awaiting me as by magic? Who was the dark, sad man in Lyon?"

"I ALMOST hate to tell you," said Barnes slowly. "And yet, Marie, you're the one person whom I can trust, and who must know the truth. For weeks, I've been sitting in front of a café doing nothing, while Rothstern's agents watched me. In that time, I've built up an organization to take the place of our own. I saw the smash coming. Good as we are, we're nothing against these double-crossing rats who call themselves secret agents."

"Apparently you've done the impossible," she said dryly.

"I have. Everybody has overlooked a great bet. For fifteen years, France has been the haven of Armenians—not the low-class peddlers we know at home, but people of the highest class. That man in Lyon is a graduate of the Sorbonne, Oxford, and Geneva. His father was an intimate friend of the sultan before the war. The man who gave you the tickets in Nice, was once a prince. These refugees have no country, no cause, no hope. I have given them all these things.

"One of them alone might betray me; banded together, they would never betray one another. They have a cohesion of blood, of race; America helped the Armenians, and they remember this. I am cashing in on byproducts of past history."

She drew a quick breath; her eyes dilated as she watched his keen, alert profile.

"You? Who else?"

"No one else—except you. I figure on keeping the wrecks of our organization and using them, chiefly as a mask. Rothstern and the like will never look beyond to seek a second-degree organization."

"Then you—single-handed—you are doing this—"

Barnes smiled thinly. "The Sphinx, my dear; the Sphinx, U.S.A.!"

"Who supplies the money?"

"I furnish some of it. Other Americans have contributed. I have friends who trust me, remember, and who ask no questions."

"Either you are an absolute madman—or a genius!"

The gray eyes twinkled at her. "Which do you say?"

"Both. Oh, it's wonderful, it's splendid!" she broke out passionately. "If only you can depend on these people—"

"I can. They have relatives, friends, all over France. They are like the Jews, a race absolutely banded together in ruin; they have an infinite genius for detail. I give one of my key men certain instructions; he arranges everything. I can hand one a message today in Paris, and it will be delivered in the most spy-proof manner that same night in Vienna, Naples, Marseilles, Petrograd—and at the same identical moment. You see, the possibilities are vast, almost unlimited."

A sobering thought. "And you see why I've picked on you?" Barnes glanced at her, laughing. "Any other woman would have been mourning her clothes, her personal possessions, everything she'd lost. You don't. You're always a good campaigner."

"Oh, we can always buy more!" she exclaimed brightly. "But don't you want that letter?"

Barnes shook his head. "Wait until we reach Dijon. It'll be in code; it was given Franklin for delivery to me, by an Armenian in Rome."

"So you're using codes, which can always be broken down?"

Barnes chuckled. "I'm using the German code system, which has never been broken down, and never will be. With an Armenian complex, it's invulnerable. You'll see." She shrugged and relaxed on the cushions.

It was nearly dark when they came into Dijon; Barnes did not want to arrive in full daylight. They avoided the grand Hotel de la Cloche and in a side-street off the main Rue de la Liberté, halted before a small hostelry, the Hotel Burgundy.

"We become brother and sister; the name is Smith; passports

are ready in that name," said Barnes. "I'll take that letter, if I may. Meet you downstairs in half an hour."

She produced the letter Franklin had turned over, and they entered the little hotel, which had for lobby only the usual small office.

Once in his own room, Barnes tore open the letter, which contained a single sheet of paper. On this were three lines of unbroken typing in capital letters.

In ten minutes he had reduced this to the "cable-ese" of newspaper correspondents, which he then amplified into familiar English. The result was very definite:

BALKAN TENSION HOLDING UP ABYSSINIAN CAMPAIGN BUT PREPARATIONS GOING STEADILY FORWARD. LEAGUE OF NATIONS WILL CONTROL JUGO-SLAVIA. AIRPLANE FLEET PREPARING HERE FOR LONG FLIGHT.

Mussolini had once sent a squadron of twenty-odd ships across the Atlantic to America. He would be able to send a fleet of fifty bombers to Eritrea to act against the Ethiopians. No particular news here; Franklin might have lost this message without any dire consequences, thought Barnes angrily. Then he started, at a sudden thought. He held the paper against the electric bulb in his room. Between the lines of typing, appeared writing as the paper grew warm. He copied it swiftly, decoded this second and more secret message, then whistled softly.

MY BROTHER AT MARSEILLES INFORMS ME THAT TWO BELGIAN SHIPS CLEARED FROM THERE FOR BOMBAY. REALLY FOR DJIBOUTI WITH IMMENSE QUANTITIES WAR SUPPLIES CONSIGNED ADIS ABEBA.

There, by glory, was something!

DJIBOUTI WAS the French port of Somaliland, whence the railroad ran to Adis Abeba, capital of Abyssinia. The French, then, were permitting war supplies to go through, in defiance of all conventions. Why? Stumbling block. And Marie Nicolas had heard talk of those two ships. Belgian ships; and the Belgians had furnished drill-masters for the Abyssinian army. Something here, something big, if only the key could be obtained.

Hastily washing up, Barnes went downstairs and found Marie awaiting him in the lobby. They left the hotel; they were going to dine, he told her, at the Grande Taverne in the Rue de la Gare, near the railroad station. Reilly, if he got through alive from Paris, was to meet them there about eight.

"It is a risk meeting him, of course, but it must be done," said Barnes. "He has the key to all this business. Now, listen to what was in the letter," and he swiftly sketched the contents of the missive she had brought.

"What does it mean, then?" she asked.

"I don't know. That's what Reilly can tell us. Washington is involved somewhere; so is half Europe. Abyssinia is helpless, but has money to burn—an important point. Well, here we are."

The entered the café, took a corner table within view of the door, and settled down to satisfy hunger.

"Where did you leave the car?" asked the girl.

"In the street, handy for a quick getaway. Whether we'll stay the night, I can't say. Depends on Reilly and Rothstern. Our fat friend isn't so slow, you know," Barnes added thoughtfully. "We're taking chances stopping at hotels. By this time, our registration slip is at the police prefecture. Rothstern might figure you for Dijon, of course. We're bound to take chances any way you look at it," and he shrugged.

"Have you anyone here? Any of your friends?"

"No."

Dinner arrived. As the meal drew to its close and eight o'clock came and passed, Barnes grew more and more uneasy. Then the door opened; a gangling man with flaming red hair and clipped mustache entered and glanced around. He sighted Barnes, who rose.

"Hello, old chap," said Reilly. "Ah! And Marie as well, eh? Glad to see you enjoying life. You won't very long."

He dropped into a chair and fired a rapid order at the waiter, who vanished.

"Trouble getting here?" asked Barnes.

"Nothing else but. I've been driving that old Ford of mine over half the back roads in France. You know what's happened to the gang?" Barnes nodded. He liked this brisk, energetic Chicagoan.

"Sure. But we're not washed up yet. What have you for me? Spit it out."

"You're welcome to it," said Reilly, and grinned. From inside his hat he brought a small envelope. "And, by the way, you'd better be prepared to hustle. Ten miles out of town they caught me. I rammed their car into the ditch, but it'll mean that the net is spread here."

Barnes took the envelope and looked at Marie. "Sorry, comrade; you'll have to wait to get the news. Will you slip back to the hotel, get my suitcase put into the car, and drive the car here?

"Tell the hotel people we're going to join friends at the Hotel de la Cloche. The rooms are paid for."

With a quick nod, the girl rose and swung away. Reilly looked after her; his face was suddenly drawn and tired.

"A swell girl, there," he said. "I'm done for. I'll stop here and let 'em grab me."

"You will not," said Barnes quickly. "You'll go with us. What's this thing?"

He tapped the envelope as he put it out of sight.

"PHOTOSTAT OF an agreement between Rothstern and that chap Forville, in the French Foreign Office," Reilly said crisply. "Cost me a thousand bucks cash, but I got it a week ago. Forville will be made the goat if it should become public, of course; the French government is really back of it. Ever hear of Abyssinia?"

"Once or twice," Barnes replied. "Anything to do with war munitions?"

Reilly chuckled. "You're not so slow, huh? Right. Here's the layout—hold on."

The waiter came with the ordered dishes. Reilly, saying he had not eaten since morning, pitched in ravenously. When the waiter was gone, he spoke between bites.

"For three months, Rothstern, on the basis of this secret agreement, has shipped munitions into Abyssinia. Made money hand over fist at it. That Italy's going to grab the country is no secret. France is bitterly jealous of her already; so is Germany. Mussolini is all burned up over the disaster of Adowa, forty years ago, and means to avenge it. Well, he's going to run into another Adowa, that's all. The Italian army will be smashed; his prestige will never recover. Rothstern is behind the whole thing. A gigantic trap in the mountains.

"Get the picture? France then becomes the dominant power in Europe, and so forth."

"Holy smoke!" exclaimed Barnes, as he comprehended the reality. "What's it got to do with Washington? We don't give a hang about Abyssinia?"

"Sure," grunted Reilly, "they've hung it on the Paris ambassador; he thinks it's swell. The Abyssinian envoy has let it be understood that America will guarantee the integrity of Abyssinia; which is all rot. But they've got Rothstern scared stiff about it. So the fat boy wants to find out about that treaty. He thinks we might stop Italy from grabbing; more rot. He wants Italy to grab, burn her fingers, and take a tumble."

"I get you. What good is this photostat to us?"

"Proof. Our diplomatic corps doesn't dare touch it; the thing was swiped out of the French archives, you know. But any of us can handle it, with the fervent blessing of Washington. If Mussolini gets it, he has proof that France is double-crossing him. You knew I was bringing you orders to meet Grimaldi in Ostend, on neutral ground?"

"No! I was told to meet our ambassador there and take the treaty to London."

"All hooey, brother. You're to do it, sure, but the important thing is to meet Grimaldi. He's Mussolini's best friend. We didn't dare reach him in Paris; you can do it in Ostend. Give him the photostat—on condition Italy won't grab Abyssinia. If Grimaldi assents, Il Duce will probably stick to it."

Barnes saw the whole thing now. If Italy held off, that commercial treaty might or might not go through. All this was a job that no accredited diplomat could handle for a moment. Grimaldi, not the American ambassador, was the real work ahead of him.

"I get you. Grimaldi might not agree, though."

"He will if you tell him that Italy gets a fifty-fifty split in the treaty, and a concession to build a railroad into Adis Abeba. The black boys will probably repudiate the whole thing, even if Washington makes the treaty, but we should worry. Our game is to smash Rothstern—wheels within wheels, savvy?"

Barnes nodded. "What a whale of a scheme! It saves Abyssinia's independence and yet profits all concerned. Who thought it all up?"

"Those blacks aren't so dumb," and Reilly grinned. "Look here, you'd better skip out! Leave me here to act as decoy."

"Nothing doing. Come along. Marie must be outside by this time," and Barnes beckoned the waiter.

He paid his bill, and a moment later the two men left the restaurant together.

As they went out the door, a man rose from a table on the other side of the room, and made an abrupt signal. Two other men joined him, and all three hurriedly departed.

CHAPTER IV

PLAYING THE MOST
DANGEROUS GAME

REILLY, CROWDED into the roadster seat with Barnes and Marie, continued his sketch of the situation as Barnes headed out of the city.

"You see, once the proof is in Grimaldi's hands, he's got Rothstern by the neck. And believe me, Mussolini would like to see that bird done for! France will have to sacrifice Rothstern, and so will Germany. They won't dare let him squawk. That's added incentive for us. We owe him something. Where you heading for now?"

"Troyes," said Barnes. "I'll have a man waiting there for me with news, food and anything else needed—including gas. We'll get there long before midnight. Then on to the Belgian border."

"I can't cross it," said Reilly. "You had better let me go."

"Be hanged to you!" Barnes snapped. "I'll manage it somehow."

They got out of town without incident and the powerful roadster began to eat up the miles of the highway, as the rolling hills of Burgundy fled past.

"Light's behind!" said Marie Nicolas, presently.

Although Barnes knew the road, it was strange to him at night; a hilly road with sharp curves and blind turns. Speed was impossible. Gradually the following car lights crept closer.

"Looks like a pinch," commented Reilly. "And those birds will shoot. They shot at me; that's why I rammed them off the road."

Barnes reached down with one hand, drew a pistol from the car pocket, and laid it in his lap. "This stuff has to get through," he said grimly. "If we're nabbed, you two step out and give up. You'll only get a week in jail at worst. Orders, understand?"

The minutes passed. That the other car was the faster, now became all too apparent. Barnes reflected swiftly, and came to a decision. Alone, he might outrun or outfight the enemy, no matter which; they were not French police, who would use pistols only as a last resource. But with Marie in the car, he could not risk her life so freely.

"Be ready to pile out," he said curtly. The other car was close now, its lights holding them in full glare.

Barnes slowed gradually. He ran along the edge of the road, giving plain evidence of his intention to stop. There was still a chance, of course, that the other car held nothing but tourists or fast travelers who wanted to pass. A "honk-honk" from behind as the pursuing car closed in and began to pass. It came alongside, roaring along without slowing. Then—

The jets of fire, the crashing of the windshield, the barking explosions of pistols. A wild cry from Marie.

Sheer blind fury seized Barnes. The whole windshield in front of him was shattered out. Glass flinders stung his face.

Like a flash, he stepped full on the gas, snatched up his own pistol, and as the roadster spurted into a roar after the other car, he began to fire. Shot after shot, steadily, always in the one place. Suddenly a scream drifted back to him. Then a chorus of voices. The car ahead veered, skidded off the road, went slap-bang into a tree with a terrific crash. One of his bullets had found the driver.

The roadster shot past. Barnes looked back once, saw no flames, and grimly held his course. To hell with them! They could take the consequences, so long as their car had not caught afire.

"Marie! Hurt?"

"No, no," came her gasp. "But Reilly—you'll have to stop—"

Barnes slowed, and presently ran to a stop. Like all European cars, this one had a right-hand drive. Thus, the other two had acted as shields for him against those bullets. And one had found Reilly. The red-headed Chicagoan was dead—had died at once, for a bullet had gone through his head.

"What'll we do?" exclaimed Marie, careless of the gashes in her arms from the shattered glass. "We can't leave him here."

"No. You drive. I'll hold him. We're well on our way to Troyes. I'll leave him with my man there, who will take care of it. The body can't be shipped home in any case; anyone who dies from violence must remain buried in France. That can all be taken care of later. The main thing now is to get on." They went on.

I T WA S a grim ride. Barnes sent his thoughts flitting ahead, groping with what might lie across the border. No such danger from the police as here. The whole French bureaucracy was riddled with graft and corruption and scandal; Belgium was another thing. He could understand why Reilly had held this photostat for days, no doubt in the hope of getting it to the Italian embassy, but in vain. Rothstern had paralyzed the little band of American volunteers.

For Rothstern knew of this photostat. What an incredible devil of mental agility, of information, of secret sources, that fat man must be! He had learned of this. He knew his own peril. He even knew—or guessed—that it was to reach Grimaldi on the Ostend musical expedition.

Barnes voiced his thoughts, as Marie sent the roadster roaring on. She had the whole story in her mind, now.

"If I'm stopped, you must carry on," he said. "The photostat is in my inside right coat pocket. You must put through the deal if I fail. Understand?"

"Yes," she said simply. The one word held volumes.

"Get the thing straight. Rothstern probably knows what I don't know—that I'm picked to meet the American ambassador in Ostend and carry that treaty over to London, where it can be sent in the diplomatic pouch without danger. That arrangement is of course a mask. I'm to meet Grimaldi, or someone is, with this photostat and make the deal. And Rothstern surely knows of the photostat."

"But you're to meet the American ambassador too?"

"Naturally. That can be done openly enough, without danger. There is probably going to be a whole diplomatic gathering at this musical affair next Friday. Which reminds me—I must arrange about tickets. It'll be held at the Kursaal, of course; that's the big concert place in Ostend. My man at Troyes will attend to it."

"Are you going to explain that code to me?"

"Yes. The minute we have an hour to ourselves. Over the border."

"Shall we get over?"

"We must."

Troyes was at last on the horizon, and the ghastly ride was presently at an end, and poor Reilly at peace. This was in a furtive little street behind the Hotel Terminus, where a plump, gray-bearded man and his two sons saw to everything. He put into the roadster a hamper of food and wine, and when Barnes introduced the girl to his unpronounceable name, he bowed to her like a courtier.

"*Mademoiselle,* I am honored. You behold but a damned dirty dog of an Armenian, as they called me at Eton in my youth; yet we Armenians may have our uses, eh? Here, Mr. Barnes, are telegrams. One, I fear, will cause you sadness."

They drove on, Marie taking the wheel while Barnes looked at the telegrams.

"I suppose," she asked, "that man was a prince or something?"

"Eh? Oh, not at all," said Barnes. "He was a multi-millionaire before the war. Look here! McGibbons was killed today, in Warsaw. An automobile accident."

"McGibbons?" she echoed in dismay. "Sandy McGibbons? Oh—"

"Exactly; one of our best men. Accident? Not a bit of it." The voice of Barnes was grim. "Now we've come down to murder. Poland, remember, is a close ally of Germany in the new alignment. Our other news isn't so good, either. Truxon left Nice today and landed in Paris this afternoon, by air; Stacey was with him. Rothstern went on by the same train from Lyon to Paris. Gave you up as a bad job, evidently. Once we get out of town, I'll drive. Tired?"

"Not a bit," she lied bravely.

Troyes fell behind.

A meal as they drove, with hot coffee and a dash of cognac from the hamper, made the cold night look different. Spare gasoline was in the luggage compartment; later, they filled the tank. It was a mad, wild flight through the morning hours; dawn found them speeding forward, with Marie huddled up asleep. Sunrise at last, and in the golden morning they railed up to the frontier station of the Douane, and Barnes adroitly conveyed a thousand-franc note to the customs inspector in a packet of cigarettes.

Ten minutes later they were in Belgium, unhindered; even the broken windshield had drawn no suspicion.

"Now what?" asked the girl.

"On to the city of Mons. Then hotel; sleep; rest; buy whatever we need. No hurry," and Barnes uttered a gay, joyous laugh. "To-day is Wednesday. We'll stop here till morning, get the windshield replaced, and drive on to Ostend tomorrow. Comrade, we've done it!"

"At a price," she murmured. Barnes lost his cheery air; his face darkened.

"Right. Let me tell you something; when I fight fire with fire, I don't use water. Rothstern murdered Reilly and McGibbons, and that signed his death-warrant. You can pull out of my game if you don't like it. Fair warning!"

She eyed his harsh, strong features with their hint of savage determination, and nodded. She made answer with quiet restraint.

"You're not the man you were; not the same. You're getting bigger, if not better. You're going far. And I'm trailing along, thanks."

"GOOD GIRL. You know. I've got something to fight for; we both have," broke out Barnes with sudden deep feeling. "Back home, these callow university pinks, these agitators, these damned communists who never heard of patriotism, say that Americans have no cause, nothing to fight for, no reason for loving country. Wait and see. By God, I'm going to carry things home to these murdering rats over here! This organization is now mine. I'm going to use it in my own way. And everyone else be hanged!"

"Good for you!" came her voice, low, vibrant, rich. "You're not afraid to do things; right or wrong, you do things. Most men don't, any more. They're afraid to make mistakes, afraid somebody will call them down. Ugh!"

"And let me tell you one thing," Barnes said, tapping her on the knee. "Your report on that conversation in the hotel in Nice—girl, that's big! It's going to change everything, all my plans. It shows me a lot. We'll not go into it now, for my brain's dead. By the way, take this photostat, won't you? Pin it under your dress and carry it; I'll feel safer."

"All right, Mr. Sphinx," she said, smiling, and the precious thing passed into her keeping.

Mons grew ahead of them at last, in mid-morning. Ten minutes after they arrived, Barnes was asleep. For the present, worries and cares were left behind.

That same evening, after Barnes had dispatched a sheaf of telegrams, they visited a movie together in delicious relaxation and safety. A good night's sleep followed. With morning, they were off, driving unhurried through the rich Belgian fields. The wild and frenzied flight north was like an evil dream over and done with.

Before reaching Ostend they halted for dinner, in order to delay their arrival until after dark. Marie Nicolas, getting a postcard, demanded a fountain pen.

"Haven't one," said Barnes. She stared at him blankly.

"But you have! What's that clipped to your waistcoat pocket?"

Barnes grunted, drew out the pen to which she referred, and replaced it.

"That," he said, "is a little improvement of my own on a parlor toy. Waiter! *De quoi eécrire*. Well, Marie, this time tomorrow night either you or I should be hearing the Beethoven Mass and talking business with Grimaldi. I've instructed all my agents, by the way, that you're second in command."

"Oh! But—do you know you haven't explained that cipher?"

Barnes whistled. "Right! Later on, then. It'll take time. Get your postcard off and we'll be on our way."

OSTEND, THE glittering Atlantic City of the Belgian coast, opened before them. Ostend, the cheap and flashy, shopworn with years and British trippers. Barnes, as usual, avoided the big hotels and drew to a halt before a small and unostentatious hostelry half a block from the "board walk," as it would be termed in America.

"Behold the Belgian Lion!" he exclaimed gaily. "Warranted a cheap, inconspicuous, and small inn. As soon as we get rooms, will you chase out and find me a stenographer?"

"I'm one," she said.

"I must have one who can put English or French into Italian, which I don't know."

"I speak Italian perfectly."

Barnes broke into a laugh. "Good! We'll dispense with the stenographer."

They secured rooms on the same floor. Half an hour later, Barnes finished his dictation. He took the photostat, which he had requested from Marie.

"Doesn't it seem rather silly to have only one of those?" she asked.

"Precisely," and the gray eyes twinkled at her. "I'm going out now to find one of my men and have another made. Then we'll each have one. I've decided to let you conduct all negotiations with Grimaldi."

"What?" Her gaze widened on him. "But you—"

"Will be throwing Truxon off the trail. The performance begins at eight tomorrow evening. At seven, two tickets will be delivered here; the two seats next Grimaldi, his wife and secretary. You'll take them and go, presuming nothing happens to prevent you. If I don't show up, you'll have an empty seat beside you.

"Make an extra copy of that dictation and leave it for me, if you don't see me in the morning, at the hotel desk. Take your own copy with you. First, is the contents of the photostat; give that to Grimaldi and get his instant attention. Then give him the terms on which he may have the photostat—the second dictation. If he signs these, give him the photostat and the game's finished."

"But you—"

"What? Are you going around all your life repeating those two words?" demanded Barnes. "Me, I've got to see the American ambassador in the afternoon, let Truxon and possibly Rothstern follow me around, and maybe buy me off.

"Who knows? I'll shove the photostat under your door if you're asleep when I get back."

"I was trying to tell you," she retorted, "that you can't have a copy made at night."

Barnes regarded her with lifted brows.

"You might tell me, also," he rejoined, "that it is impossible to get, from the eye of a dead man, the picture of his murderer. In both cases, you would be wrong—quite contrary to general belief. I'll go into the matter scientifically with you the next time we find a murdered man and no clue to his killer. Meanwhile, my dear, enjoy yourself, keep off the streets, and don't talk with strange men. *Au revoir!*"

He departed, with a grin, leaving her half angry, half perplexed.

An hour later, after a long conversation with a lean, dark man whose curio shop-window bore the startling name of Djismardahossian, Barnes went to one of the largest hotels in Ostend. No other, in fact, than the singularly named Hotel Delicious. Here he displayed himself prominently about the lobby, registered, secured a room, went to his room and turned in for the night.

"She can handle Grimaldi better than I can anyhow," he reflected cheerfully, as he switched off his light. "And I'm the bird they're all out to catch. So, with luck and one stone, I'm liable to kill two birds and prove that the hand is quicker than the eye. Good hunting tomorrow, Rothstern—damn your black heart!"

When Marie Nicolas wakened next morning, she found an envelope shoved under her door. In the envelope was the photostat. On the envelope was the rubber stamp of The Sphinx, U.S.A. But she saw nothing of Barnes that day.

CHAPTER V

A STRANGE SUDDEN END

AT THREE O'CLOCK on Friday afternoon, Barnes was ushered into the presence of the American ambassador to France, who by some curious chance was also stopping at the Hotel Delicious. The diplomat looked worried, and he was worried.

"Barnes, this damned nonsense must stop," he exclaimed, in the undiplomatic language of big business. "Your wild-cat organization is busted. These European crooks have got the whole crowd by the tail. Reilly's dead. McGibbons is dead. Others are in jail. You must give up the whole show; it's come to an end."

"On the contrary," said Barnes coolly, "it's just begun. If you think two boys like Reilly and McGibbons are going to be bumped off, and nothing done about it, guess again. The crowd's busted, sure, just as I predicted it would be. I'm running the show with a crowd of my own, now."

The other gave him a keen, angry glance.

"You're in earnest?"

"Absolutely and entirely, sir." The level glance of Barnes was like gray steel.

"You're a fool. These secret agents are dirty, double-crossing, treacherous rats. Men like you can't hope to fight 'em."

"Terriers wipe out rats," said Barnes. "Me, I'm the damndest terrier you ever saw, right now. This time tomorrow I can walk down the boulevards in Paris and the police will tip their hats to me instead of trying to grab me. Wait and see."

"You're a blasted ass. Europe is in a ticklish condition. None of us in the service can be responsible for you. If you get in a jam, you're without appeal. You've no connection with Washington. Damn it, I admire you with all my heart, but—"

"You stick in the embassy and I'll play the small-time circuit," and Barnes grinned. "What you don't know, won't hurt you. With Marie Nicolas and a few of the old gang, I'm going ahead; you might tip off the other appointees from Washington to this effect. Now, I'm in a bit of a rush. Do you want me to take that treaty draft over to the London embassy?"

"Yes. It's blasted important too." The ambassador extended a sealed envelope.

"Wrong; it'll die a-borning," said Barnes. "I've learned something about it. This treaty is a blind to get Europe all het up over America's butting into the African game. Abyssinia would repudiate the treaty even if we bothered about it, which we won't."

And he departed, leaving the ambassador frowning after him, more worried than ever.

BARNES LEFT the hotel. He strolled over toward the plage, the wide expanse of sands, villas, bathing huts, stretching up to the massive concrete harbor works. He paused at a café, seated himself with a sigh, and ordered a Rossi. It was just four o'clock. He squirted the glass full of seltzer water, pinched the slice of lemon peel into the blood-red mixture, then sipped at it contentedly and watched the passing throng.

Ten minutes later a large, beaming, jovial figure came swinging along, stopped short at sight of Barnes in well-simulated astonishment, then came to his table.

"My friend, Mr. Barnes, of all people!" exclaimed Rothstern, cordially. "May I sit down"

"Why not?" Barnes said. "Trailed me, have you? No use lying about it?"

Rothstern chuckled, as he seated himself and ordered a beer. "I suppose not. We need not lie to each other, *hein?*" He wiped his bald spot and beamed. "Well, like you Americans, I shall get down to business. Come, Mr. Barnes, we need not be unfriendly. You are going to England; would not a little English money come in useful over there?"

"A little? No," said Barnes curtly. "A whole lot might, though."

Rothstern heaved with laughter. "Ah, you Americans! Come, my friend. I will make you an offer," and his voice dropped until it was barely audible. "Two thousand English pounds if you will let me copy the document you received from the American ambassador. No one will ever know. It will take ten minutes."

"You think I'd sell out? To you?"

"Yes," said Rothstern blandly. "Remember we have met before; you were ready enough to take my money then. Why not now? The cash is ready. We need only step over to my hotel. Why should we not remain friends, to the advantage of both?"

The gaze of Barnes lowered. "Hm! Maybe you're right, Rothstern. If what I hear is true, the game is up for most of us Americans, anyhow."

"Ah, my boy! With Papa Rothstern your friend, who knows? Come. Finish your drink, step to the Grand Hotel with me, and in fifteen minutes—*pouf!* It is over."

Barnes kept his eyes veiled, to hide their hot agitation. So plausible was the man that he might have been fooled, had not Marie Nicolas overheard the actual intention of Rothstern, had he not known who was responsible for the deaths of Reilly and McGibbons. Abruptly, he tossed down his drink.

"All right," he said with decision. "But I'll not walk over with you, naturally."

"Oh, as you like!" Rothstern rose. "Come in five minutes. Take the elevator to the fourth floor; I'll be awaiting you in the corridor. So long!"

He swung away with a wave of his malacca stick. Barnes looked after him, eyes narrowed, cold, implacable.

Five minutes later, Barnes rose, paid for the drinks, and walked toward the Grand Hotel. The die was cast now; he was gambling everything on one turn of the cards, almost literally. As he had told the ambassador, it was make or break this same night.

He had no illusions whatever about Rothstern's intentions, or the trap laid for him.

The Grand Hotel, with its gardens and spacious lobby, opened before him.

He walked steadily to the elevators, took a car up, and left it at the floor designated. Rothstern was waiting.

"Ah! You are wise, my friend, very wise; I welcome you," said the fat man with hearty cordiality. "Come along. I have every-thing ready. Here is the room—" and he flung open the door of a corner room, with a laughing bow.

Barnes, with a slight shrug, walked in. The door closed behind him. At one side stood Truxon, at the other the rat-like Stacey, each with a pistol in hand.

"Hello," exclaimed Barnes. "Why not a machine gun? I thought this was a private affair, Rothstern."

"An excess of zeal, perhaps—merely to make sure you are not armed, my friend," purred Rothstern. "You do not object?"

"Not in the least." Barnes held up his arms. Truxon, he of the lean and savage features, stepped forward and frisked him—efficiently.

"So that is finished!" exclaimed Rothstern. "Now we shall all be friends, Stacey! Go and get the motorcar ready for us. Mr. Truxon, you will remain, if Mr. Barnes has no objection?"

"I have," said Barnes coolly. "Our talk is to be private."

"Very well." Rothstern turned, and winked significantly at Truxon. "Go into the adjoining room, and wait. But leave the door open, mind! Come, Mr. Barnes, we can settle matters comfortably at the table."

STACEY DEPARTED, with an air of disappointment. Truxon, scowling savagely, went into the next room of the suite. Rothstern showed his victim to a chair at the center table, himself taking a seat opposite.

"Now," he said, rubbing his hands, "first, the treaty draft. Here, I have paper ready,"

"And the money?" asked Barnes in a cold voice.

"Ah, yes! The money, of course." Rothstern:reached into his pocket and brought forth an envelope, which he handed over. His gaze was greedy, excited, nervous. Barnes produced the sealed envelope which the ambassador had given him; and Rothstern snatched at it, broke the seals, drew out the folded paper. "Ah, this is it!"

"Of course," said Barnes. "You want to copy it. Here's a pen."

He took the fountain pen from his pocket—then froze abruptly. Rothstern's hand jumped forward, covering him with a pistol. The fat, jovial features were suddenly cruel, tense, deadly.

"Hands there on the tahle—that's right!" cried Rothstern. "All right, Truxon."

The latter appeared, giving Barnes a quick, cold grin.

"So, my very good friend!" snarled Rothstern viciously. "You think to play with me, eh? You think to take my money and go? Not so quickly, young man. You have a lot to learn. You have other things I want to see; what about your meeting with the Italian ambassador, Grimaldi? Yes, I know about that. You're helpless. You're in my hands now; I have the treaty entrusted to you. Be careful, or I can ruin you!"

"Rothstern, you're a good actor," said Barnes coolly. "Trying to work me, are you? Trying to force me to cough up all I know—and then you'll kill me. Oh, don't deny it. What about your instructions to Truxon and Stacey, that night you met them in the hotel at Nice?"

Rothstern started. His eyes distended a trifle. "Ah! *Herr Gott!* How do you know that?" he muttered thickly.

"Never mind. No time to discuss it," Barnes rejoined. "I've only time to remind you of something, Rothstern. You're a damned murderer. You were behind the death of Reilly, of McGibbons, just as you expected to be behind my death."

"Well?" The gaze of Rothstern bored into him, no longer jovial, but wicked and cold with hatred. "What of it?"

Barnes shrugged and looked down. "I'm just reminding you, that's all. Suppose you go ahead and copy the paper."

And, casually, he unscrewed the top of the fountain pen and laid it down. Then he leaned back in his chair, produced a cigarette, and lit it, with an air of perfect unconcern.

Rothstern stared at him for a moment, as though trying to figure out his attitude. Then, putting the pistol on the table at one side, Rothstern emitted a grunt.

"You damned American swine!" he said slowly. "Ah, if I could only have mv way, all of you would go—would go—"

He swallowed hard, opened and shut his mouth spasmodically, then fell back in his chair. A little sigh escaped him, and his chin sank on his breast.

"Good God!" cried out Truxon. "A stroke—"

With the word, Truxon darted forward, caught at the pistol, shoved it into his pocket, then leaned over the crumpled figure of Rothstern. He glanced up suddenly at Barnes, who had not moved. What he read in the face of Barnes, brought him erect.

"You!" he cried out. "You devil—"

His hand went to his pocket. Like a flash, Barnes was out of his chair, flinging himself forward—too late! Truxon had no idea whatever of using a pistol here in the hotel. A supple "persuader" leaped out in his hand. As Barnes came into him, he struck, struck once and with the swiftness of light.

Barnes went down like a shot and lay on the floor beneath the table, face to the carpet, senseless.

With a scornful oath, Truxon straightened up, then once more leaned over and caught Rothstern by the shoulder and shook him. He looked down and saw the paper in the hand of Rothstern. His eyes dilated upon it. There upon the paper was a scarlet rubber stamp—the figure of a Sphinx.

"So that was it!" muttered Truxon. "That was what—what—"

He caught his breath suddenly, turned, started for the door; but he did not reach it. Barnes came to himself presently. His eyes opened, as he lay there with his face against the carpet. For a moment he lay quiet. His gaze swept the floor. He saw the feet of the dead Rothstern, and over near the door he saw Truxon outstretched, both hands gripping at the carpet.

Then, without rising, Barnes drew himself away from the table, little by little. There was a trickle of blood on his cheek, and his head was swollen. Truxon had not spared strength in that blow. Presently Barnes gathered himself, came to one knee, and rose. He went to the nearest window and opened it, not without difficulty, for his head was swimming. He turned and looked at the room again.

"So! He knocked me over—and put me in the safest place of all," he murmured, and a thin, hard smile touched his lips for an instant, and was gone.

He took from his pocket the envelope of Bank of England notes Rothstern had given him, and made a gesture of repugnance. He crossed to where Truxon lay, and felt the man's limp, dead hand. He took the notes from the envelope and pressed the dead fingers hard about them; he kept the envelope, which bore his finger-marks. Then he came back to the table, reached out gingerly, and took up his fountain pen. He screwed the cap in place and pocketed the thing.

"Executions by gas," he observed, his voice striking low and sharp upon the terrible silence of the room, "are still a novelty—in Europe."

"There's your warning, Europe!" he said grimly. "Tell 'em all your story, Rothstern; chancellories, police, detectives, secret agents, cabinet members—tell the whole blasted crowd your story! They'll understand, right enough!"

III

THE SPHINX STRIKES

The Calais to Paris express carried a dead man—and that meant a danger-fraught task for America's master spy.

CHAPTER I

DEATH ON WHEELS

FOUR THINGS happened on a bright spring day in the year 1935. Let us consider three of them, apparently unrelated. They will tie into the fourth later.

In one corner of a compartment of the most luxurious train in Europe, the Golden Arrow, bound from Calais to Paris and the Riviera, sat a young man with a New York newspaper across his lap. He sat with his head back against the imitation lace headrest, his eyes closed. He looked rather pale, and was alone in the compartment. This was odd, since tickets above each seat showed them all reserved; he must, therefore, have reserved the entire compartment. On the seat beside him was an open port-folio, or brief case, stamped with his name in gold: Howard Charteris. On the floor at his feet, as though escaped from his fingers, was a portion of a torn envelope. As it lay, part of the address could be read:

> *Mr. John Ba…*
> *Hotel V…*
> *Pa…*

When the door of the compartment was sharply slid back, Charteris did not stir or open his eyes. A man stepped inside. A slim, young, dark, and well-dressed man, who spoke abruptly.

"Mr. Charteris! I've come for the message for Mr. Barnes. I must warn you—"

Barnes fired across the gas-filled room.

He broke off, leaned forward, touched Charteris on the shoulder; his black eyes dilated abruptly. Charteris did not move. A sharp gasp escaped the young man. He caught at the hand of Charteris. It slid from his grasp, rocked back into place.

The black eyes touched on the open portfolio, then fell to the floor. The dark features changed. One slim hand swooped, picked up the fragment of envelope.

The other hand clutched at the open brief case and held it to view. An American passport, a bundle of letters in a rubber band—nothing else.

With incredible agility the visitor slid the door open, stepped

*It was the Japanese who had been
trailing the American.*

out, closed the door and was gone. The dead man in the corner
made no protest.

That was one thing.

UNDER THE trees that surround the Théâtre Marigny,
just off the Champs Elysées, in a drizzle rain, a seedy old man
in rusty black clothes walked up and down, moodily glancing
at one of the most curious sights in all France, which may be

seen on the afternoon of every Thursday and Sunday in the year, rain or shine.

The old man was stout, gray-bearded, and bore a remarkable resemblance to the last Sultan of Turkey, Mahmud VI, may Allah bless his happy exile! It is whispered that there are reasons for this resemblance. This man, in his day, had won or lost a hundred thousand dollars at a sitting without turning a hair, and had owned palaces which could vie with those of the Sultan himself; for, once upon a time, there were rich Armenians. Now he looked sadly in need of a haircut.

The rain did not spoil things for the children under the trees; on wooden benches their gleeful outbursts of shrill voices rang forth continuously. Two puppet shows were here, Thursday afternoon being the French holiday, and children thronged them. On past the puppet shows were hordes of umbrellas, where at the corner of the Avenue Gabriel were set up booths. The crowd was solid, thick, impenetrable. This was the Stamp Bourse, where collectors of postage stamps, dealers, sellers and buyers, thronged as they had thronged for sixty years and more.

Many of these pathetic merchants in little things were Armenians, for at this business the men who had no country were very apt. Hundreds of thousands of francs changed hands here each holiday.

The old man glanced at his watch, turned, then quickened his pace. Coming toward him from the Champs Elysées was a young fellow in the blue, red-tipped uniform of the Bureau des Postes—that is to say, the postal service, in which France comprises telephones and telegraphs as well as letters.

The two met and halted.

"Here they are, my uncle," said the young fellow in uniform. "Five telegrams all told. These are the originals. It cost me five thousand francs to bribe the clerk of the records."

The older man took the sheaf of bluish telegraph forms and stuffed them into his pocket. From a wallet he produced five beautiful lavender banknotes of a thousand francs each, which the young man hastily tucked out of sight, then a sixth.

"There, my nephew," he said in Armenian. "You have done well. Those telegrams will drink blood—the blood of an American who betrayed his country."

The two parted. A couple of Englishmen, swiftly striding, cloaked in Burberrys, sticks swinging, came past. The old man almost collided with them. They glared at him.

"Damned dirty dog of an Armenian!" said one, and went on.

The old man looked after them, fingered his gray pointed beard, and chuckled softly.

"Yes; a damned dirty Armenian dog," he repeated, mouthing the words unctuously. "So much the worse for you, Englishmen. It took an American to discover that dogs have teeth."

That was the second thing.

I N   A handsome room of the handsome American Embassy, which enshrines the memory of the greatest American Ambassador in France since the days of Franklin, sat two men smoking cigars; aggressive, dominant men. One was very angry.

"Damn it, this man Barnes is stark, raving mad!" he declaimed. "He'll embroil us with half of Europe before he's through. He sticks at nothing. He laughs at my authority. I threatened to withdraw his passport, and he dared me to try. He has more infernal gall than a newspaper man! He seems to think I'm nothing!"

"Compared to him, you're not," said the second man, with a cool laugh. "Nor am I. You're only an ambassador, old man. He risks his neck."

"Oh, I know all that," impatiently. "But why doesn't he risk it decently, in the accustomed fashion?"

"Because he's too damned smart, Barnes is."

The angry man grunted.

"A month ago the whole French police were after him. I was

requested by the Prefecture to wash my hands of him. Now he's here in Paris, openly."

"Doesn't that suggest something to you?" asked the cool, amused man. "Better wake up to it, old chap; Barnes is one hell of a guy, and no mistake! You're not responsible for him. He has no connection with Washington; officially, he's nothing."

A telephone on the table buzzed sharply. With a word of apology, the angry man lifted the instrument and replied. His face changed.

"I've done nothing as yet," he said. "We suspect a certain member of the staff, but of course cannot act without some proof…. What? *What?* Do you presume to give me orders as to my actions?" His face reddened. "Yes. He just arrived from Geneva… Oh, you do?" He turned to his visitor. "Barnes wants to speak with you."

The second man leaped up, seized the instrument, responded. Then, with a word of thanks, he set it down on its rack and whistled softly.

"Good Lord! He's sending me over the complete text of the secret Russian agreement with China, in case of war with Japan. How the devil did he get that? Made some swap with Moscow, I suppose. Man, oh, man! Look here—what got you so upset?"

The angry gentleman cursed.

"Says he'll uncover that leak in the embassy here, the one that's bothered us so long. Told me to do nothing about it."

"Then, do nothing, like a wise chap." The other resumed his cigar, puffed at it, and faced his host gravely. "Look here. Some time ago we all thought we were smart, when a dozen or so Americans with money, brains and knowledge started out to serve us as unofficial spies. They were patriotic. They were willing to meet these damned European diplomatic agents on their own ground, fight fire with fire. And what happened? They're washed up, wiped up, half of them dead. Fleming's in jail now in Berlin, and we can't do a thing about it. Of them all, Barnes still is in the game. Why? Because he cut loose. He's running a show of his own, with Marie Nicolas and a couple more helping him.

"Howard Charteris has resigned from the London Embassy and is coming over to pitch in with Barnes, I understand. A good man, Charteris—"

The telephone buzzed again. The angry man, still angry, responded. He made a curt assent, and hung up. Then he turned.

"That was the Sûreté speaking. They've just been informed that an American with a diplomatic passport has been found dead aboard the Golden Arrow, due in at seven from Calais. They want me to send over one of the staff to meet the train and comply with the formalities. It's murder and robbery, apparently, for he was stabbed—"

"Who?" demanded the visitor. "Who's the man, damn it?"

"Howard Charteris," said the Ambassador grimly. "Now prate about your confounded smart Barnes, will you?"

CHAPTER II

A FATAL SLIP

THE FOURTH thing was a slip of paper.

The Hôtel Vignon is far behind the Madeleine, in the short little street of like name—a tiny hotel unguessed by Americans or tourists. Barnes had his own reasons for stopping here, on the second floor. It was a discreet place.

Twice, John Barnes had seen the girl in apple-green. Once, last night, in the downstairs room that served as office and lobby, and once in the elevator. Now, as he approached the hotel entrance after a brisk afternoon's errand, raincoat flapping about his legs, he saw her again. She was just entering the hotel ahead of him.

His gray eyes quickened, his lean, hard features softened. She was a thing to gladden any heart. The swift, lithe walk, the delightful figure, the high, confident carriage; a face unutterably lovely, with fearless, tender eyes of warm lights, and soft ash-blond hair. An American girl, yes.

Barnes

Barnes had no interest beyond swift appreciation of her beauty, her appeal. When he came into the hotel, she had just closed the little elevator door. He took his key from the rack and mounted the stairs with rapidity to the second floor. He saw her there, leaving the elevator and passing down the hall ahead of him. She halted at a door across from his but a little farther down the hall.

As Barnes inserted his own key in the lock, he heard her cry out—a quick, sharp little cry. He swung around.

She stood as though frozen, staring down at something. She shrank back, saw Barnes, and extended her hand. Her voice came with quick appeal.

"Please—look at this, look! Do you speak English? It—it can't be—"

Barnes hurried to her side and looked down. From beneath the closed door crept a slowly widening pool of dark red. His eyes bit at her.

"Who's in there? Your husband?"

"Husband? Of course not." Her voice was steady enough. "Nobody. I'm all alone. But that must be blood—"

Barnes tried the door. It opened to his thrust for an inch or so, then stopped, as though checked by something inside.

"Oh!" she exclaimed, holding up her key. "And I left it locked, too!"

Shoving harder at the door, Barnes got a glimpse of the interior.

Then he pulled the door shut and turned to her.

"Go downstairs again, right away. Go into the dining room and order a drink of some kind. Wait till I come down. You're an American? My name's Barnes. Let me take care of this matter for you."

She met his regard, and nodded. The quiet words of Barnes, his cool eyes, his harsh, thin features, inspired confidence. Without a word she turned and departed.

Good girl! She had sense. And what loveliness!

When she had gone down the stairs, Barnes put his weight on the door, forced it back, and stepped into the room.

ONE GLANCE showed him what had happened. The man had entered and had stepped on a thin, slithery rug that went out under his feet. Falling heavily, without warning, his head struck against the foot of the iron bed.

A nasty gash over his temple. Quite dead. The blood trickling slowly away and under the door. Entirely obvious, except that the gash did not quite fit any projection of the iron bed that Barnes could see. However, this did not matter—at the moment.

A hotel rat; a slim, rascally fellow, well dressed. In his hand was still gripped the skeleton key which had won his entry. Barnes frowned. Why the devil had a thief entered this girl's room? He knelt, wrapped a handkerchief about his hand, and carefully went through the fellow's pockets. He turned up nothing except some brass and copper money, and a slungshot. Nothing else—except that crumpled bit of paper at one side, fallen from the man's left hand, no doubt.

Barnes picked it up, glanced at it, and whistled softly. He tucked it away, then glanced rapidly about the room, looked into the dresser drawers, looked into the unlocked suitcases. Coolly, without scruple, he investigated the private affairs of the girl. A little bundle of letters from New York, addressed to Miss Anne Warren, care the American Express, London. A passport in the same name, with her picture. He glanced through it. She had landed at Cherbourg two days ago; had come from London. An American girl, of course. He looked through her effects, which were pitifully meager. Little money, it seemed. Some music. A music student. A letter of introduction to a French pianist, from a music house in London.

He left everything as he had found it and closed the door, then went into his own room. This room had the only telephone in the hotel. When he had left his coat and hat, Barnes went downstairs and walked into the dining room, on the right of the entrance, where the girl sat at a table. A waiter came; Barnes ordered a Rossi, and then nodded at the anxious, questioning eyes opposite.

"Not so bad. Does any one know you went upstairs?"

"I think not. No one was in the office. They pay no attention." She smiled a little. "By the way, I forgot to introduce myself. I'm Anne Warren. I'm going to study music here. I have a letter to a great pianist—Santos Fleurien. I haven't much money, but he may take me. Does that explain me?"

"Admirably." The gray eyes of Barnes warmed on her lovely features. "As for me, I'm an occasional dealer in precious stones; I happen to have some now. There's a rug in your room, a flimsy blue rug—"

"On the linoleum floor." She eyed him in startled comprehension. "I've slipped on it twice when entering. You don't mean—"

Barnes nodded. She knew about that rug, then? At the moment, he shrugged off the question.

"This fellow slipped, went down heavily, and struck his temple against the foot of the bed. It killed him. He's a hotel rat, a sneak thief."

"But what shall I do?" Her eyes dilated. "I've heard terrible things about the police in France."

"They're all right. I see you have a package there. Call the manager and ask him to send it to your room—say you must go right out again. The *garçon* will take the package up, will discover the unlocked door and the body. It's simple."

Her brows lifted slightly. "But I handled the doorknob. So did you."

"I wiped off any fingerprints."

"But why should he have entered my room? I've nothing worth stealing."

HER EYES compelled him. Their intimacy, their appeal, warmed him; this girl was like an old and dear friend, all at once. The subtle flattery of her obvious liking, of her trust, her helplessness, reached into him. He got out the crumpled bit of paper he had found, and spread it out. She glanced at the three figures on it, and frowned.

"One seventeen. What does that mean?"

"Everything. The man dropped this. A Frenchman writes a one with a distinct serif. He writes a seven very much like a four; therefore, to distinguish it, the seven is always crossed on the vertical stroke. But this was written by an American, who wrote a straight vertical stroke for the one, and did not cross the seven. He wrote 'One Seventeen,' which is the number of my room. This hotel rat was a Frenchman, He took it to read one fourteen, which is the number of your room."

"Oh!" Comprehension flashed into her face. "He was looking for your room, then!"

"And the precious stones there." Barnes glanced at his watch. "May I suggest that you go to the office, get the manager, and beat it? Don't come back for an hour. Then you'll find a detective from the Sûreté, detective headquarters, waiting to question you. Tell a straight story, know nothing, and you're all set. We might walk up to the corner together—I have to meet a man."

She assented. Barnes paid for the drinks while she talked with the manager. He joined her at the entrance and they walked together up the street toward the boulevards, and parted at the corner. She gave him her hand and her eyes; her fingers had a caressing touch that made his heart leap. She was so obviously innocent of coquetry, so fine and lovely.

Then she was gone, toward the Madeleine and its gay flower-market. The rain had ceased, but early darkness threatened. Barnes, bareheaded, had only half a block to go. He turned in at a boulevard café and took a corner seat on the long leather lounge that circled the sides of the place. Close to him, at the next table in fact, was a seedy, stout man with a gray beard, who looked much like Mahmud VI of Turkey. It was the *aperitif* hour, when everyone in Paris sought a drink before going home to dinner. The old man was sitting dreamily over a coffee and brandy, staring at nothing with moody eyes. Barnes ordered a vermouth, and when the waiter was gone, spoke under his breath.

"Any luck?"

The old man fingered his beard dreamily. His voice came very softly. "We got them. They're on the seat beside me with the paper. When I'm gone, take up the paper and you'll have them. A man is watching you. He came in after you and is sitting at the table next the cashier."

The speaker put a coin on the table, pressed his hat on his head, and rose. He walked out of the café. Barnes yawned, and as the waiter returned with his drink, leaned over and picked up the folded *Paris Soir* left by the old man. As he opened it out, five folded telegraph forms slid into his lap and under cover of the newspaper were slid into his waistcoat pocket. The waiter set down his drink and departed.

HE HAD them! He had them! The end of weeks of long planning, of careful work; here was triumph at last! Over the newspaper his gray eyes touched on the man indicated. He received a shock. This man was a Japanese, a conspicuous person in Paris.

Two men, laughing and talking, swung into the place and took the recently vacated table next to Barnes. They were dark, swarthy fellows, conversing in a strange tongue. The waiter took their orders and departed. They never so much as glanced at Barnes, but he, behind the newspaper, spoke casually.

"Get word to Miss Nicolas that I must see her at nine this evening. I'll come to her apartment. Have it well watched and a taxicab waiting in the street at nine-thirty."

"*Entendu, m'sieu'.*" The words came clearly amid their jargon. "Understood."

Barnes went on reading. After a moment he caught a few words in English.

"Eramian has wired that he must see you. The man from London was dead."

"I heard of it from the Prefecture," responded Barnes. "Tell Eramian to be in the taxicab. Did he learn anything?"

The two men called for a backgammon board and began their game.

"He did not say. He will arrive at seven with the train," said one of them after a moment.

"Very well. Have the Golden Arrow met, every passenger noted. Whoever did it must be on that train. Send word to me at the apartment of Miss Nicolas."

"Understood."

Presently Barnes finished his drink and sat reading the newspaper. The Japanese was still there, inscrutable, motionless. The minutes flitted past. Darkness had descended on the streets outside, with promise of more rain.

A man entered briskly and looked around until his eye fell upon Barnes. Then he came over, shook hands, and settled down on the red leather. The two men at the next table finished their game and departed. This newcomer was a Frenchman, alert, gimlet-eyed, polite, with a subtle air of authority.

"*Mon ami,* we are ready to deal with you," he said amiably.

"Thanks for the condescension, Flandreau." Barnes grinned. "What's happened to make you see reason?"

"The last straw. Germany, England and Moscow have received an accurate report of our secret arrangement with your President regarding the gold accord. Somebody has betrayed us. We must work together."

"So?" The brows of Barnes lifted slightly, giving him a sinister, mocking air. "Flandreau, do you by any chance know just whom you're working against?"

"Certainly," Flandreau replied with assurance. "Baron von Bohm, the German agent. He acts for both Russia and Germany. We are watching him. We do not deport him because by watching him we'll get a lead to all those connected with him. You see, I am frank."

"And yet you have need of me?" Barnes laughed heartily. "Come, Flandreau, be yourself. You're up against it. You don't know whom to suspect. The baron is a figurehead. He doesn't represent Germany or Russia. The truth is, you're up a stump. You know that any day, any time, but probably before the year's out, Germany goes monarchist, Hitler is shot or escapes by his secret plane—and France is up against something new. And you don't know who the devil is pulling the strings; but I do—a man sitting in this very room."

Flandreau gave the American one sharp, almost desperate look, then his eyes flitted about the place. He turned to Barnes.

"You're not joking?"

"I'm not. What's more, I know who's sold you—and us—out. I think I've got the proof of it in my pocket. Do you want to talk business—and no camouflage?"

"Yes," said Flandreau in a low voice. His gaze was intense, searching.

Barnes took out pencil and paper. From his waistcoat pocket he slipped forth one of the five telegrams, unfolded it, and copied off the message upon it. The message alone; not the address or signature.

A MAN, young, dark, accompanied by a girl, came in and took the adjacent table. They were laughing and talking together; they sat side by side, the young man's arm about the girl's shoulders. They kissed, in the charming fashion of Paris, and broke into laughter.

The girl spoke in French, gayly.

"*Tiens!* And to think he is sitting outside all the time!"

Barnes cocked one eyebrow and glanced whimsically at the Frenchman.

"Apparently the young lady has a husband, eh? Or a fiancé."

"To business," said Flandreau, with an irritated air. "What are your terms?"

Barnes handed him the paper with the message.

"The assistance of your best code authority, first. This must be deciphered; then others."

"Granted. Colonel d'Aleyne shall have it instantly. He is probably the most expert man in Europe on ciphers. Next?"

"My friend Fleming is in a Berlin jail. I want him sprung and brought here."

Flandreau whistled. "Can we work miracles?"

"You must, if you work with me."

"H'm! At least, we'll do our best."

"See that it's your best, my friend. Last of all, I want a report on every Japanese who is in Paris, domiciled or visiting. The Prefecture can supply this within a few hours, if the government demands it. Well, demand it! I want it before nine in the morning, at my room in the Hôtel Vignon. Here's my card; it has my telephone number. Ask Colonel d'Aleyne to communicate with me by phone, please, as soon as he learns anything about the cipher."

Flandreau stared hard at the American. Then he turned his head and looked around the room again. The Japanese who had been sitting near the cashier's desk had taken his departure a moment previously. Flandreau frowned and pocketed the card. "You Americans!" he said, with a gesture. "Very well. I accept. And in exchange you offer—"

"All the details at my command regarding Germany—and

the threat against your colonial empire in Indo-China. Word of honor. Yes or no?"

"Yes. I think you must be the devil in person," said Flandreau. "Or, shall I say—the Sphinx?"

"I know nothing about the Sphinx."

Flandreau rose, shook hands cordially, and departed.

Barnes followed. Outside the entrance, where tables were ranged under the awning on the sidewalk, he paused to light a cigarette. His eye caught that of a bronzed, handsome man sitting by himself, who lifted a hand and hailed him.

"Hello there, Barnes! Haven't seen you in ages. How's everything?"

"Hello, Westlake. Pretty good, thanks. Still telling the ambassadors how to run their offices?"

Westlake laughed. "Oh, I'm a mere secretary, you know. I'm thinking of spending a few weeks with my sister in Geneva, if I can get leave. Why do you stick around in this beastly climate of Paris, anyhow?"

"I'll tell you," said Barnes. "It's because I've got to work in order to live."

With a nod and a laugh, he swung away. His fingers, tucked into his waistcoat pocket, touched the five telegrams that Westlake had written.

He went back to the Hôtel Vignon.

IN THE lobby, two obvious agents of the Sûreté were politely and reassuringly talking with the distressed Anne Warren. Barnes went on up to his room. He entered, switched on the lights, and glanced around. Then he took the five telegrams from his pocket and gave each one a swift glance.

"Odd!" he murmured. "Each one sent to his sister in Geneva. Clearly in code. No proof of anything here—and we must have proof."

He selected the message of most recent date, the same copied off for Colonel d'Aleyne. It, like the others, had gone from an

Auteuil office, though Westlake lived at the other end of town. It had no connection with him except that it was addressed to his sister. Thanks to this, the five messages had been discovered. It was dated a week previously. It read:

E E T E K C X K I U 4 7 T K O U

O B 6 P 6 J Q P F 4 I 5 A 5 6 0

It was signed Raoul Delisle.

As he studied it, Barnes frowned. Then he produced the slip of paper dropped by the dead hotel rat and looked at the penciled room number there. One seventeen. The seven was identical with that of the penciled message here, although the vertical stroke was crossed in the telegram. The same man had made each of those peculiar figures.

"H'm! Westlake didn't dare use a typewriter, lest it be traced," muttered Barnes. "Of course, microscopic examination might prove that this message was written by his pocket pencil; no direct proof there, either. Decode it, and we've got him."

He rang the bell and ordered dinner.

Scarcely had he finished his meal when the manager, in person, brought word that a Colonel d'Aleyne was below. Surprised, Barnes descended, met his visitor and took him up to the room. A brisk, military man with a sweeping white mustache, d'Aleyne wasted no time on small talk. He brought out the message copied for him.

"Allow me, M'sieu' Barnes, to explain to you about this cipher, which I recognized very quickly. I came personally; it was the only way."

He now produced four circles of cardboard of graduated sizes, and laid them on top of each other, smallest uppermost. About the edges of each circle were marked spaces, containing the English alphabet and numbers from two to nine. With a pin inserted through the center, d'Aleyne arranged the circles so that the letters and figures coincided. Then he revolved them so that, reading from the outermost, the word "PEER" was spelled in toward the center. All this in absorbed silence.

He produced a sheet of paper and spread it before Barnes. Upon it was typed:

3 5 X Z B G 1 4 G L D T Y

---

1 2 3 1 2 3 1 2 3 1 2 3 1

"Observe," he said. "The top line is the message in code. The letters and figures are numbered from one to three. Now these circles. The outer one is merely the static index on which the. message is read. A four-letter word, PEER, is used as the key. To read this message, the circles are arranged thus: they are numbered from one to three—beginning with the second, re-member. The outermost is only the index. Good. Look for 3 on this index. Corresponding to it, in the first circle, we have G. Look for 5; in the second circle, the corresponding letter is I. Look for X; the corresponding space in the third or smallest circle is V. Look for Z; we find opposite this, in the first circle, the letter E. We have read the word GIVE. The complete message reads GIVE ME THE WORD. You understand, now, how these circles are used?"

"Perfectly," said Barnes.

"This cipher came to be used by Imperial German Head-quarters during the war," said the precise little expert. "It is, even in this simple form, complicated. Imagine six circles instead of three, a six-letter word used as the key, and you have combinations and complications almost beyond the power of the human brain to grasp. The cipher has never been broken down, and can never be broken down unless one knows the key word. Those using it establish different key words for each day of the week, let us say. Who can guess them? The prime letter E may be represented by half a dozen letters or figures. There is no way to break it down."

"But my code message—?"

"Cannot be read unless you supply me with the key word."

"Are you positive?"

"I came to tell you this personally, M'sieu' Barnes, because I am so positive. What I have explained is the English or German cipher. If written in French or other languages with varying numbers of letters in the alphabet, we have further complications. I regret to say that you must provide the key if you want these messages read."

CHAPTER III

THE THUMB PRINT

MARIE NICOLAS had just taken an apartment near the Etoile, a very handsome little flat in a new and handsome building that glittered with light, was admirably policed and guarded, and gave no encouragement to secret visitors.

Marie herself, vibrant, alive, glowing with a dusky beauty that set men's hearts hammering, shook her head vigorously at Barnes as he sat there. "I tell you, I have contacts in a dozen places; I know absolutely that they suspect you of being the Sphinx! They're waiting to pin it on you, before killing you. I've heard twice that a trap is laid for you already."

"Before tomorrow morning," said Barnes slowly, his eyes grim and hard, "they'll hear from the Sphinx in a way they'll not like. They! This time, we're working with the French Secret Police. And nobody suspects who's working with me."

"I'm shadowed day and night," said the girl, with a shrug. "True, they don't know that you've got half the Armenians in Europe working with you. That was genius."

Barnes admitted it. "Yes. These people are extraordinary in brains and ability. They've no country. They're like the Jews in many ways; genius, genius! For America, they've got warm and splendid feelings. They're bound together so closely, there's no danger of betrayal."

The girl's eyes rested on him with warm appraisal.

"Have you any intention of telling me what we're working on just now? Whom we're against? What we're doing?"

Barnes broke into a laugh.

"Of course! We're going to nail the fellow who's been selling us out. His name's Westlake."

"Oh!" Incredulity leaped into her face. "Impossible! He's a secretary of the Embassy here—a splendid fellow, a career man in the service—"

"The last man on earth to be a traitor; so was Benedict Arnold. I've no proof. I want you to get it. His sister lives in Geneva. Somewhere in her possession is a list of code words, possibly one for each day of the week. Either four or six letter words. That's all I know. That's all I need. I must have those words."

Marie Nicolas leaned forward.

"His sister? Yes; I know who she is. Married to a Swiss manufacturer. A wealthy man."

"Will you take the job?"

"Of course. Now, what's this business of Italy trying to grab Abyssinia? I thought you had secured a pledge from Mussolini that—"

Barnes made an impatient movement.

"My dear Marie, pledges amount to nothing. There's a new factor in the game, in the whole European situation. A new, sinister, amazing factor. As to Italy, let that wait. We must nab Westlake first of all. You must get off tonight on the midnight express if possible."

"Very well," she assented. "If you—"

A bell tinkled. Barnes nodded. "Some one for me, I think."

S H E   R O S E and went to the door, admitting a young, dark, handsome man who spoke perfect English. Barnes rose as they entered the room. "Ah! Miss Nicolas, let me introduce Mr. Djissian; upon you two people hang most of my plans. All right, Djissian. Where's Eramian?"

"In a taxicab below," said the young Armenian. He extended a torn scrap of paper, on which were brought out certain finger-prints. "He found this at the feet of Mr. Charteris, in the compartment. Part of the enve-lope addressed to you. On it, there's one thumb-print we've been unable to identify."

Marie Nicholas

"Good! That of the murderer, very possibly. By the way, Marie, you knew Charteris was killed today?"

The girl paled. "Not Howard Charteris? Oh, it couldn't—!"

"It is. He was coming from London to join us. All right, Djissian. What about the people aboard the train? Any Japa-nese?"

"None, Mr. Barnes. There was, however, a Russian by the name of Protopoff, who is a friend of Baron von Bohm, and who deals in antiques. He travels often between London and Paris. I happened to follow him myself. He went home, then he visited an agency for theater tickets, then he visited that oriental café in Rue de Silz and dined there. He then went to the theater, and I came here."

"Then we've lost the message Charteris was bringing," mur-mured Barnes. "All right. The thumb-print will tell. What is this Protopoff's address?"

"Forty-two, Bis, Rue Vaurigard."

"Very well. Tell Eramian to await me downstairs. Telephone

me at nine-thirty in the morning and have every available man in readiness. That's all."

When the visitor had departed, Marie Nicolas regarded her caller thoughtfully.

"So we—or you—are working with the French, eh? And tomorrow you may be at odds with them. Then they'll know your secrets."

"Not they." Barnes smiled slightly. "I'm living openly at the Hôtel Vignon. Tonight I contacted half a dozen of my agents under the very eyes of Flandreau, their best sharpshooter; and he never got a thing."

"All right; I hope you can keep it up. So von Bohm is the man behind the scenes this time?"

"No. He's a figurehead; nominally a Nazi agent, in reality double-crossing Hitler and working for the monarchists. Europe's at peace, my dear—at peace, understand?" Barnes fastened his eyes upon her. "Under the loud talk, the war clouds have all fled. A new force has entered the diplomatic field—a force with which we are about to have a skirmish. Next month, next year, the skirmish will have developed into actual war; the two most powerful forces in the world will meet here on the field of European diplomacy. I've just discovered all this. It cost us the death of Charteris."

"What?" Her eyes dilated. "You don't mean Russia—"

"Bah!" and Barnes lit a cigarette. "Why are we making head against this army of spies, double-crossers, liars, murderers who call themselves secret agents? Because we're serving an ideal. We don't work for hire. We have no selfish interests masked as love of country. We're playing America's hand without her knowledge or consent. Good! And America is one of the two strongest forces in the world today."

"THE OTHER?" she questioned, her breath coming sharply. There was something electric about Barnes, even in repose as now. A confidence, an assurance, a knowledge. Excitement drew at her features, widened her eyes, sharpened her breasts under her thin silken gown. "The other?"

"What! You, the cleverest woman agent in Europe, haven't guessed?"

She nodded. "Yes. I've guessed, to myself; but it seemed too incredible."

"Of course. Who forced two enemies, Poland and Germany, into their present strict alliance despite France? That was bad news for Russia, you know. Who would like to grab the French colonial empire in Indo-China and Yunnan? Who caused the present strained relations between Washington and Moscow, so that in February half our Embassy staff there was withdrawn? Who's backing Abyssinia now with arms, men, and money, against the Italian grab? Who has practically isolated Russia and is working to isolate France? Just one answer. Men who serve no selfish cause, but an ideal. A great ideal, one that threatens the world!"

"Then it's true!" she murmured. "Asia—for the Japanese!"

"Absolutely." Barnes leaned back. "So far, they've been learning. They thought the game consisted of lies and bluff; they denied everything and got caught. Now they're playing better. When they're ready for war with Russia, look out! These enormous air bases in China are camouflage; they're built with Japanese money. China isn't building them, except nominally. Well, never mind all that. We're in Europe. Do you know why Charteris was murdered?"

"No, naturally."

"He was bringing me a letter that meant nothing; but in his head, the terms of a new proposed agreement between Washington and Moscow and London. Litvinoff was coming to Geneva; I was going there to meet him. Stanley Baldwin proposed it all. Well, poor Charteris is dead, and so the thing is delayed. But when they start in to murder—let them look out! They'll hear from the Sphinx now."

"AND YOU'RE sending me away. Why? To be out of the mess?"

Barnes gave her no hint of the tumult that stirred his pulses when he met her eyes, when he drank in her loveliness, her vibrant eagerness and joy in life.

"No. I'm asking you to take over the most important thing of all; to nip the man who has been selling out the United

Protopoff

States to other interests. You know that Russia has obtained those new airplane wing designs. You know that Persia—Persia, of all nations!—has given England an immense order for airplanes, but minus engines, because she has obtained the specifications of certain United States Army plane engines."

"What has Japan to do with all this?"

Barnes shrugged. "I'm talking about Westlake just now. If he could get the terms of that agreement between London, Washington, and Moscow—ah!" Suddenly he leaned forward, a blaze in his eyes. "Listen! He'll get those terms. He'll wire them to his sister, or wire her that they're on the way by messenger or by mail—tomorrow night. Do you understand? His sister will be decoding a message from him tomorrow night. Will that give you any assistance?"

Marie Nicolas nodded. "Of course. It'll help a lot."

"Then get your typewriter and take down some dictation, like a jewel."

The girl unlumbered a portable typewriter and for twenty minutes took dictation on it from Barnes. When he had finished, she regarded him curiously.

"Do you know, it's rather clever? You'll send it through the mail, eh? That means it'll pass through Westlake's hands—"

"No, my dear. That would bungle things. You'll cable it from Geneva in the morning, in the usual government code, and sign the name of our Minister to Switzerland. That means it'll pass through Westlake's hands for decoding."

"And you make me liable for forgery, eh?" Her eyes danced merrily. "Oh, my dear John Barnes—you have genius! Positive genius! I can't tell you how much I admire you. Honestly!"

"And I don't dare tell you how much I—admire you, Marie," he said softly. "I don't dare. Not now." He rose abruptly and caught up his coat and hat. "So long! Wire me, phone me, reach me somehow, the minute you get those words that I need. I'd better get on and let you pack. And better send me your Geneva address; I may need something more while you're there. Good-by and good luck."

For a moment he pressed her hand, then turned and was gone.

ACROSS THE street from the apartment house stood a taxicab.

Barnes strode to it and got in; a man was sitting in the dark of the rear seat. The cab started at once. "My cousin is driving," said Eramian. He was a thin, dark, tubercular man, like so many of his race. It was he who had entered the compartment of Charteris aboard the Golden Arrow that day. His name, if not the man himself, was known among Armenians all over the world; a name of princely, almost royal, family.

"Rue Vaugiraud," said Barnes. "That is, if you wish to go with me. The errand is not a pleasant one, perhaps. If Protopoff does not return home alone, we may have trouble."

Eramian shrugged as though he had seen too much trouble in life to be more than mildly amused by the word.

"Very well," he said, and spoke to the driver. "While we're driving across town, shall I give you the reports from our people in Berlin and Rome?"

Barnes assented.

CHAPTER IV

THE RUBBER STAMP

THE FRENCH run apartment houses with a certain system. A concierge occupies the ground floor, with a window overlooking the entry. All mail comes to the concierge. No one ascends to the upper floors without his scrutiny, at least in theory. He is a bonded employee. After ten at night the entrance is locked; the concierge opens to a pull of the bell and makes sure who comes or goes.

When Protopoff arrived home that night, a taxicab stood outside his apartment house. As he left his own cab and rang the bell, a brisk figure approached him.

It was Barnes, who spoke quietly. "M'sieu' Protopoff? I've been awaiting you. I have some orders for you."

"Eh?" exclaimed the Russian. He was a large, thick-set man of perhaps forty, and surveyed Barnes with suspicion. "I do not know you—"

"Fool! Do you want me to blurt my errand in the street?" snapped Barnes. "I need only mention the Golden Arrow."

"Oh! I understand," muttered Protopoff.

"I have a friend who is to be put under your orders," went on Barnes. He beckoned, and Eramian approached. At this instant the door-latch clicked.

"Come along upstairs, *messieurs*," said Protopoff, and led the way.

With entry accomplished in this manner, the concierge could later report only that Protopoff had come in with two other men, unknown.

Protopoff occupied the rear apartment on the first floor—the second, by American usage—whose balconied windows over-hung the street. As he came into his apartment and switched on the lights, something hit him with paralyzing force at the base of the skull. He pitched forward and lay quiet.

"Into a bedroom with him," said Barnes, closing the door of the apartment. "Then we'll make certain."

Between them, they carried the unconscious man into one of the two bedrooms, laid him comfortably upon a bed, and Barnes frisked him without making any discoveries. Then Barnes produced an inked pad. In a moment, a bit of paper held the impressions of Protopoff's two thumbs. Barnes inspected them through an enlarging glass, handed the glass and paper to Eramian.

"Look. Here's the bit of envelope you found on the train, with the impression of the murderer's thumb brought up. Compare them."

Eramian looked carefully. "Identical," he said.

"Exactly. Search the outer rooms; put on your gloves first."

Left alone, Barnes produced a rubber stamp, touched it to the inked pad, and then pressed it on the extended right wrist of Protopoff. Upon this wrist appeared in red the outline of a Sphinx, and beneath it the letters, "U.S.A."

Barnes placed the left hand of the Russian across the breast, under the chin, then from his own pocket drew a small wooden box. This was apparently stuffed with cotton; but from the cotton he carefully lifted a round object the size of a robin's egg. He placed this in the left hand of Protopoff, closing the fingers around it, and stepped back. He regarded the senseless Russian with cold, stern eyes.

"In three minutes," he murmured, "the heat of the hand will melt the wax; then the gas escapes. You murdered Howard Charteris this morning; tonight you pay the penalty of that crime."

He turned off the lights and left the room.

At a desk in the reception salon Eramian was busy. Barnes joined him. Together they went through letters, papers, everything in sight. Barnes turned up a small address book, glanced through it, and pocketed it with a nod.

"The man was no more than a messenger, a hired murderer," he observed. "Turn out the lights and come along."

He opened one of the windows over the street, which was empty of life save for the taxicab awaiting him. Barnes whistled, then his voice gave a curt order. The taxi leaped into life and noise. It came beneath the little iron balcony and drove up over the curb to the sidewalk, directly beneath the balcony.

Barnes climbed over the rail, let himself down until he hung by his hands, and dropped the three or four feet to the top of the cab. Eramian, after closing the window, followed him.

A moment later the taxicab was rolling away.

The Sphinx had come, had struck, and had gone.

WHEN BARNES reached the Hôtel Vignon—afoot now—midnight was at hand. In the tiny office was sitting a man reading a newspaper. It was Flandreau.

"Ah, my dear Barnes!" he exclaimed, jumping up. "I've been waiting for you. We may, perhaps, go to your room?"

"By all means," assented Barnes, taking his key off the rack and nodding to the sleepy *garçon* behind the desk. "No mail for me, Pierre?"

"Two letters, *m'sieu'*."

Barnes pocketed the letters and took Flandreau up in the lift to his floor. He ushered the secret agent into his room and switched on the lights. Flandreau glanced around quickly, took the chair indicated.

"You asked for a list of all the Japanese in Paris, by nine tomorrow morning," he observed. "I have it for you now. The American, Fleming, held in a Berlin jail, has been released tonight on condition that he leaves Germany at once. He left Berlin half an hour ago by plane for Paris."

Barnes stopped short, staring at the other.

"By plane!" he echoed slowly. "There's no regular night flight. Did he charter a plane?"

Flandreau nodded. "A Dutch Fokker. Why?"

The American dropped into a chair, lit a cigarette, and shook his head.

"Flandreau, I'm pretty much a failure," he observed. "I've bungled things badly. Afraid this isn't my game. I jump at conclusions and act on them, instead of waiting for solid bases as you chaps do."

The other laughed. "My friend, you belittle yourself. By the way, what do you know about the man who was killed tonight just across the hall?"

"Eh?" Barnes glanced up in surprise. "Nothing. I haven't been here. Who was killed, and why?"

Flandreau regarded him curiously, smiling a little.

"A sneak thief, apparently. He happens to have been one of our own men who was in the employ of Baron von Bohm. His death was most unfortunate—for us. So you have not been here? Then forget it. I thought you might cast some light on the matter.

"By the way, can't you give us some line on the Sphinx? He seems to be an American."

"I only wish I could," murmured Barnes. Then, to hide the swift flash in his eyes, he got out his two letters and tore at them. So that man, sent here by Westlake apparently, had been a French spy—then it was no accidental death whatever, but sheer murder!

No wonder the wound in his head had not fitted the bed-end at all.

Barnes unfolded the papers in his hand. A letter, and a carbon copy; both of them startling enough. He moved over to his desk, with a word of apology.

For a moment he bent there, his back to Flandreau.

Then he rose and came forward, smiling.

"This gave me a bit of a jolt," he said, holding up the carbon copy and reading it swiftly. His gaze jerked to the Frenchman, and he extended the paper. "Here. Half the payment I promised you; apparently accurate details regarding the hidden German air bases recently established—"

Flandreau came out of his chair in a burst of incredulous excitement. His eyes dilated on the paper. At the top was the scarlet imprint of the Sphinx, U. S. A.

"Name of a little black dog!" he ejaculated. "This—if it's fact—"

"It is," said Barnes sadly. "Fleming got it all. This came via Sweden to me; they don't know he got the information out of Germany. They think he's got it in his head. That's why he won't reach Paris alive. Better get out to Le Bourget air field with your men and meet that plane from Berlin—and see how plausible the account of his death en route will be. Go ahead. Keep the letter."

Flandreau caught up his hat and was gone on the run. Barnes followed him to the stairs, then turned and came back toward his own door.

SO THAT fellow had been a French spy, keeping von Bohm covered; and he had been sent here via Westlake; and his death was not accidental. If he had been found dead in the room of Barnes, it might have been bad—perhaps. No, that wasn't it. What the devil was behind it? Marie Nicolas had warned him. Something was up.

A bar of brighter light across the dim-lit hall as a room door opened. A figure appeared. It was Anne Warren; a light silk gown was flung over her pyjamas. She came close to him, smiling, eager.

"Oh! I was reading; I heard your voice," she said frankly. "I had to thank you for—for everything. It was just like you said. Things went off all right."

"Naturally they did," said Barnes. "All's well, then?"

"Perfect." Under the thrust of his eyes, she flushed a little.

She was lovely, adorably lovely, ash-blond hair framing her face like spun glitter of moonlight. He was conscious again of her warm friendliness, of her appeal. All unconscious that she was actually brushing against him, she looked into his face and smiled.

"Perfect," she repeated. "Thanks to your advice. I can never forget it. If it hadn't been for you—well, I don't know what would have happened, Mr. Barnes. You see, I don't even speak French very well! And guess what's happened? Tomorrow afternoon I'm to see Santos Fleurien!"

"Who's he?" asked Barnes. "Oh, I remember! The pianist. Is that right?"

"The greatest piano teacher in the world!" she exclaimed, her eyes dancing. "But I'll have to get an interpreter. He doesn't speak English, and my French is awful. And if he takes a dislike to me, he won't even think of taking me as a pupil, so I'll have to have somebody—oh! Why not you? Could you go with me and talk to him?"

"Of course," and Barnes laughed. "But suppose I scared him off? He might take a dislike to me."

"No danger," she returned. Then her face fell. "But you have business—and I'm to be at his studio at two-thirty sharp—I can't let you spoil the whole afternoon—"

Barnes patted her hand. "My dear, it's a pleasure," he said, and impulse drifted on him. They were so close; her eyes were shining with so rich and friendly a light; he had the feeling that—

For an instant his lips touched hers; he felt the answering kiss, the swift, soft clinging of her arms, the yielding—then she was gone, laughing, gaily dancing away down the corridor with a wave of her hand. Her door closed.

BARNES WENT into his own room again, momentarily intoxicated. He went to the telephone and picked it up, and called a number. After a moment came response.

"Hello, Djissian! Still up, eh? In front of the hotel in ten minutes."

"Understood," came the response.

Barnes spread out a newspaper on his desk. He made a neat little bundle of the rubber stamp and ink-pad, the five telegrams, the letters he had received; he went to his desk and added a few things from it. Then he slipped rubber bands about the whole, and went downstairs, and out to the street.

The slim, dark figure of the young Armenian appeared there. Barnes handed him the package.

"Take care of this as usual. Tomorrow noon at the Wagram Café. Send word that another telegram will probably be sent tomorrow, noon, afternoon or evening, from the same place to Geneva. I must have a copy of it."

"Understood," murmured Djissian, and was gone down the street.

Barnes went back to his own room, undressed, and got into bed. The day's work was done. As to Fleming—well, he had already made up his mind that Fleming would not reach Paris alive.

The morning papers bore the word. An American business man, en route from Berlin by air, had died from heart failure. Barnes read the short account sadly. Out of all the little band which had started off so bravely a few months back, as diplomatic free-lances, he was almost alone now. A new deal in diplomacy, they had called it, putting themselves, their money, their abilities, to work, unrecognized by their country and with no official status. Barnes remained, and Marie Nicolas; but she was supposed to be in the pay of Italy. So she was, nominally.

"The old guard of spies, assassins, double-crossers and seducers has struck back pretty hard," thought Barnes. "We pulled off some good coups; and in return—well, murder is murder. And for the moment the Sphinx has 'em all jittery. No word about Protopoff, eh? Probably his body won't be found till this morning. That will make 'em all stop and think."

NO SIGN of Anne Warren that morning. At noon, Barnes was ensconced in a corner of the Café Wagram for an hour, writing letters, enjoying a leisurely luncheon, and transacting business of various natures. The adjoining table was occupied by an animated couple, utterly absorbed in their own love affair. When Barnes had finished his letters, certain of which bore the stamp of the Sphinx, he returned the rubber stamp and two of the letters to the next table.

"To be delivered personally," he said under his breath. His eyes roved about the sidewalk tables outside; at one of these sat a slim, phlegmatic Japanese. "That's the man at the corner outside table—he gets the one that has no address. A Jap. I don't know who he is. I'm leaving the hotel about two o'clock with a lady. Better have Eramian trail me. And you attend to trailing that Jap."

"Understood," came the brief word. Presently the couple rose and departed.

Barnes finished his luncheon, studying the list of Japanese in Paris, with all the notes which the Prefecture had on each. Diplomats, students, business folk; not very many, but of a high class as a rule. Like the Armenians here in France, the Japanese were usually of wealth, good birth, or education. At length, with a shake of his head, Barnes folded the list and pocketed it. His other letters he laid aside in a pile, to be posted at the *tabac* on the corner.

"That's the same chap who was tailing me last night," he reflected, with a glance at the brown man outside. "Now it's his turn. From the address to which he goes. I can make a good guess. And by evening, I'll probably have his name. These Armenians are devilish shrewd—Oriental against Oriental, this time!"

And he smiled thinly, a briefly cruel glint in his eye. He was still smiling when a stout gentleman swung in and took the adjoining table. As he sat down, his voice came briefly, rapidly.

"Police put him aboard the plane. The pilot was a distant

relative of Baron von Bohm, whose wife is Dutch. The pilot was at von Bohm's apartment this morning and has left Le Bourget with his Fokker."

Barnes nodded. From his pocket he took a sealed letter that was addressed to Baron von Bohm, and laid it with the others to be mailed.

CHAPTER V

THE CURIO SHOP

SANTOS FLEURIEN, the teacher of piano, was a man of massive build and wild tangled hair and beard. He was an untidy man, in an untidy, upstairs apartment above an old shop on the Quai des Agustins, not far from Notre Dame, on the left bank. He was very gracious to Barnes and to Anne Warren and belied his evident reputation by charming politeness.

His apartment was small, consisting only of a large studio room and a bedroom. While Anne Warren played two or three pieces at the grand piano, and the master listened with appraising mien, Barnes used his eyes.

"Good!" exclaimed the maestro with beaming approval. He shook hands heartily with the flushed, excited girl, and with Barnes. "Good! Begin your lessons tomorrow, my dear; at the same hour. Or stay! Monday, two-thirty. Eh? Agreed."

They departed. In the street below, Barnes beckoned a taxicab and put the girl in, congratulating her warmly.

"But it was all your clever speech," she protested. "Get in, get in! You're not coming back with me?"

"Sorry, my dear." Smiling, Barnes held her hand for a moment, met her lovely innocent eyes. "I must take the Metro to Auteuil immediately—the quickest way. We might dine together this evening, to celebrate the auspicious beginning; eh? Shall we meet, say, at seven-thirty?"

"At the hotel? Good." Impulsively, she drew him forward, pressed her lips to his for one laughing, excited instant. "There! I owe you so much; I can give so little! Until tonight, then, dear friend."

The taxicab rolled away. Barnes, striding toward the corner, watched until it was lost a block away—then turned swiftly and retraced his steps.

Little old shops were crowded flush against the narrow sidewalk. He came to the stairway mounting to the studio of the pianist; below it was a music shop with unwashed windows, and beyond a Japanese curio store, the windows filled with gaudy trinkets.

Barnes mounted the stairs, swiftly, lightly. Above, he did not ring the bell of the piano teacher, whose engraved card was tacked above it in lieu of a sign. He tried the door and found that it opened to his hand. He looked in, cautiously. The studio was empty. He stepped in. The door to the bedroom was closed. Barnes went to it, cautiously opened it, glanced in. The bedroom was empty.

Barnes crossed to an open desk near the window that overlooked the Seine. He stood there for an instant, then swung around as the telephone jingled. He caught up the receiver and imitated the gruff, heavy voice of the piano teacher.

"Well? What do you want?"

"Ah, Heinrich!" came a man's voice. "Listen; it is Karl. Something terrible has happened. Tell the baron that I've just received a note of warning from the Sphinx. I must see him this evening. I'll come up to the studio about seven-thirty."

"Good," said Barnes, and the other rang off.

HE GLANCED around the room, went to a large framed portrait set in the wall, and listened. With his knife, he deliberately cut the canvas at the edge of the heavy gilt frame, and set his ear to the slit. A murmur reached him; the voice of the piano teacher, but too far away to catch any words.

Barnes left the studio and descended again to the street, a feeling of exultation rising within him. Standing on the sidewalk, he produced and lit a cigarette, then waited. Heinrich, eh? Odd name for a piano teacher who called himself Santos Fleurian! Who was Karl? Obviously, the only person to whom the Sphinx had sent a warning note this day—Baron von Bohm.

"Getting warmer!" thought Barnes, as a taxicab curved in to the curb.

He stepped into the taxicab and found Eramian on the back seat.

"Any word from Djissian?"

"Yes. The Japanese he followed, who followed you, was the clerk in the curio shop back yonder. He is now back at work there."

Barnes still had his list of the Japanese in Paris. In a moment, he came upon the name of the proprietor of that shop on the Quai des Agustins—one Harunobi, who was an art dealer, had been in Paris three years, was unmarried. The next name was that of his clerk, Sanjei Michito.

Leaning back, Barnes closed his eyes. He mentally juggled the bewildering array of facts, pieces in this game of chess which meant life or death. Baron von Bohm, who had caused the murder of poor Fleming; who had caused the murder of that fellow in Anne Warren's room. Why in that room? By mistake? Not a bit of it.

"Drive to the Prefecture," he told Eramian. "There, try and get hold of Flandreau, special agent of the Sûreté. At once!"

Eramian gave the orders. Barnes closed his eyes again, juggled anew.

Von Bohm was in cahoots with Westlake and just now was scared by the note from the Sphinx. Karl—that was von Bohm. Heinrich—who was Heinrich, if not Santos Fleurien, the great pianist? And who, then, was the baron whom Karl von Bohm must see at the studio this same evening?

Ah! Of course. As the cab halted, Barnes opened his eyes, sat up, and stared at the outer precincts of the ominous Prefecture. Eramian had disappeared up the stairs.

AFTER A moment the Armenian reappeared, hurriedly, and came to the taxicab.

"He is coming."

"Then disappear," said Barnes. "Reach Djissian immediately. He is keeping five telegrams; have him copy them, without names of the addressee, and bring the copies to the hotel—at once! Haste is imperative. I'll be waiting downstairs. Tell him that the moment the sixth telegram is sent, this afternoon or evening, to rush it to the hotel."

"Understood," said the dark man, and faded away into the passing throng. A minute later the brisk, precise figure of Flandreau appeared. Barnes was standing beside the cab, and Flandreau came up to him.

"Ah, *mon ami!* You wish to see me?"

"If you're free. Yes? Then come along." Barnes spoke to the cab driver. "To the Hôtel Vignon. Wait outside; perhaps for a long time."

In the cab, Flandreau surveyed the American narrowly.

"You look uneasy, my friend. I suppose you know nothing of the latest escapade of our mutual friend the Sphinx? In connection with the demise of a certain Protopoff?"

"How should I know anything about it?" Barnes shrugged. "Flandreau, I'm in a hole; I need your help. I'm gambling on certain information reaching me today."

"I am at your service," said Flandreau. "Presumably, you know what happened to Fleming? I have been unable to reach you—"

"I know, yes. But there is something you failed to tell me." Barnes got out his list of names and pointed to that of Harunobi. "This art dealer is a Japanese noble, a baron. What is his real name?"

"I do not know," said Flandreau. A flame rose in his eyes. "Ah! You cannot mean—"

"He is the man higher up," Barnes said simply. "Chew on that."

THE VEHICLE passed the Madeleine, turned into the little Rue Vignon, and halted before the hotel. Two men were standing beside the entrance—two men, smoking, gesticulating, discussing something or other with much vehemence. As Flandreau passed in ahead of him, one of these men spoke; Barnes paused, took the paper thrust at him.

"The telegram, *m'sieu'*. It was sent half an hour ago."

The paper burned in his hand as Barnes followed Flandreau inside. Westlake had taken the bait! Marie Nicolas had sent the wire from Geneva—and Westlake had fallen for it! Then his sister in Geneva must, even now, be hard at work decoding that message.

Barnes got his key and spoke to the proprietor at the desk.

"Mademoiselle Warren has returned?"

"But yes, *m'sieu'*, half an hour ago."

With a jerk of his head to Flandreau, Barnes sought the stairs. The two men strode down the hall. Barnes was laughing. He turned suddenly, at his door, and spoke loudly, his voice ringing with triumph.

"Flandreau, I tell you I'll have everything! The papers will be in my hands at seven-thirty tonight! It's the most important thing that ever broke, I believe. The full reports, with names, addresses, everything."

"*Mon Dieu!* Are you mad?" murmured the Frenchman. Barnes winked at him.

"No, no. I've a dinner engagement at eight. With a lady—the most charming lady imaginable! I'll have everything with me. Suppose I drop in after dinner at the Prefecture—say, at nine or a little after?"

"Very well," said Flandreau, and passed into the room as

Barnes held open the door. He swung around, as Barnes followed him and the door slammed.

"Hello! So you suspect spies about, do you?"

Barnes nodded. "Of course. Sit down for a moment, till I make a copy of this."

He went to his desk, opened it, copied the telegram; it was addressed to Westlake's sister in Geneva, like the others. When he had finished, he gave the copy to Flandreau.

"Hang on to that; I'll have others for you in a few moments. I want you to send them all to Colonel d'Aleyne, with word to expect the key words from me at any moment. Have you a messenger close by?"

"I can summon one, yes," said Flandreau, frowning.

"Do so, then," and Barnes pointed to the telephone. "You and I are going to make a social call, as soon as you send these to d'Aleyne."

FLANDREAU TELEPHONED. Barnes led him downstairs again, and scarcely had they reached the little office than Djissian appeared. Without a word he handed Barnes an envelope, and departed. In the envelope were copies of the five telegrams.

"What the devil!" exclaimed Flandreau. "Is all Paris serving you?"

"Of course," and Barnes laughed a little. "Clumsy but efficient. I carry nothing that would make my death worth while. Now, the moment your man arrives, we can be on our way."

"Where?" demanded Flandreau.

"To see Baron von Bohm. I want him removed from activity."

"What? And spoil all my careful plans—"

"Your plans be damned. I told you he's only a figurehead. Don't you know Japan is mixing in European politics? Don't you know that she wants a monarchy restored in Germany, so that Russia may be—"

"For God's sake hold your tongue," burst out Flandreau, with a startled glance at the proprietor behind the desk.

Barnes chuckled, and flung a look at the dark, swarthy hotel man.

"My dear Flandreau, the gentleman yonder is an Armenian. One may always trust Armenians—"

"Always? Never! Never!" muttered Flandreau. "What do you want to do? Raid von Bohm's apartment?"

"Immediately. Before the Sphinx has a chance to kill him."

"Oh!" said Flandreau, and blinked rapidly. "Upon my word, you may be right! We can arrest von Bohm at any time, of course—"

"Then let's do it. Now."

CHAPTER VI

A DEATH THREAT

VON BOHM was a suave, courteous gentleman who accepted his arrest with a shrug. In his pocket was found a note signed with the red emblem of the Sphinx:

> You have twenty-four hours to leave France. Return and you follow Protopoff.

Flandreau, lifted his eyebrows over this. Barnes gave the prisoner a smile.

"So you won't keep your appointment with the baron this evening, eh? Or with Heinrich, either? I fear the baron will blame you for carelessness, friend Karl."

The German's jaw fell at this.

"Herr Gott!" he exclaimed in amazement. "If Baron Hayashi—" Then he realized the trap, and stopped. Too late. Barnes grinned.

"Baron Hayashi, eh? Much obliged. Now for the telephone."

The afternoon was half gone. None the less, when he got the embassy on the wire, he found Westlake there.

"Barnes speaking, Westlake. Look here, if you'll be free for a bit this evening, I'd like to get hold of you. Something's come up that might be of great interest to you. Would you be able to drop in at the Hôtel Vignon—say about nine? Thanks very much."

He hung up, glanced at his watch, and nodded genially to Flandreau.

"Sorry; I must run. Better keep him incommunicado until morning, Flandreau. You're returning to the Sûreté? There's just a chance that I may want to reach you in a hurry."

"I'll be there until seven," said Flandreau. Barnes met the frowning gaze of the unhappy Baron von Bohm, saluted him, and departed.

Upon reaching the hotel, Barnes was surprised to find Eramian waiting in the office. This was unusual; except at his order, his men were to avoid the hotel.

"You here? Anything wrong?"

"Yes."

"Come upstairs."

When his door was shut, Barnes took the telegram Eramian handed him. It was quite incomprehensible, being in Armenian. He glanced up inquiringly.

"From my uncle in Berlin, Mr. Barnes. Announcements of your sudden death in Paris have been prepared and sent out to all Nazi newspapers for publication tomorrow."

"So? Just as they did before Dollfuss died so suddenly, eh? In that case they were correct in their prophecy," murmured Barnes.

Eramian was agitated. "I must warn you not to ignore this," he said anxiously. "God knows, your life is essential to the work. If they plan to kill you tonight—"

"It is because they expect to profit by it, to get important papers or other information from me," and Barnes smiled. "Old man, you're right. Tonight we make a cleanup—I hope. It's a gamble. Be outside in your cousin's taxicab with three other men at seven-thirty. I'll give you an address; all five of you go there. You should find two, or at most three, men who are waiting to kill me. Instead—kill them. As for the consequences, that's your gamble. It'll mean no more than a few days in jail, if that much. Are you willing or not?"

"Yes," said Eramian. "But you—"

"I'll be elsewhere. This time, the Sphinx strikes, and strikes hard; it's a matter of life or death, so let them look to it!" Barnes was hard, cold, stern. "They've chosen the weapons of murder, and I'll meet 'em halfway. I want Djissian and three or four other men on the Quai des Agustins at eight o'clock, with a taxicab waiting. At the same place I visited this afternoon. Let them be ready for anything. Have you an ink-pad and rubber stamp of the Sphinx? Give it to me." Eramian handed over a little packet which he had carried in readiness. Then he departed.

SCARCELY HAD he gone, when the *garçon* of the hotel came to the room with two telegrams. Barnes tore at one; it was from the American ambassador in London.

> Much disquieted over confidential reports from English sources. Urge you to be very watchful.

Smiling a little, Barnes tore at the other. Then he started; a glow came into his eyes. This was a longer message, also in English:

> Sunday love obey fear palm over hand rate please be careful heard rumors today am uneasy.

It was signed by the name Marie Nicolas used in communicating with him. Here under his hand were the key words—one for each day of the week beginning with Sunday. In a flame of exultation, Barnes caught up his telephone and called Flandreau at the Sûreté. Presently he had the French agent on the wire.

"Barnes speaking. Take down these seven words: the first is for Sunday. Please get them to Colonel d'Aleyne instantly," and he repeated the words. "*Mon ami,* did you ever hear of Benedict Arnold? I perceive you have. I invite you to be in my hotel room a little before nine tonight—about eight forty-five. I'll either be dead or be there by nine. And you may profit by the occasion. Eh?"

He laughed and hung up. His thoughts went to Marie Nicolas, exultantly.

"Ah! What a girl, what a girl! She came through magnificently. She can do miracles, that girl. Rumors in London, rumors in Geneva, press reports in Berlin tomorrow of my death—hm! I'm an important person all of a sudden. Charteris murdered, Fleming murdered, Barnes murdered; then they'd have a clear field again. So Westlake used a four-letter key word for each day of the week, eh? Just as d'Aleyne thought. But now we must make sure that Mr. Barnes has the information they want—"

He took down the telephone again, for some time gave directions, then hung up and left the room and the hotel. He went straight to the café on the corner of the Grand Boulevards, took a conspicuous table.

Presently a man appeared, a handsomely dressed, bearded man, who came to Barnes' table, shook hands, and sat down. He produced a large envelope, heavily sealed. Barnes counted out a thick sheaf of thousand-franc notes and in exchange took the envelope. He broke the seals, glanced at the contents, and shook hands again delightedly. The other departed. Barnes stowed the envelope in his inside pocket and buttoned his coat. Then he ordered a few sandwiches, despite his dinner engagement, and ate them. It was close to seven o'clock when he went back to the hotel, sought his room, and dressed for the evening. Not in evening dress, however. He donned black tie and tuxedo, and in the coat pocket slipped what looked like an automatic pistol—but was not.

The heavily sealed envelope he threw into his waste basket.

PROMPTLY AT seven twenty-nine he stepped down the corridor and rapped at the door of Anne Warren. The girl herself opened to him, with delighted greeting.

"You are prompt!" she exclaimed, with her air of eager happiness. "Where are we going?"

"That is for you to say," responded Barnes.

"All right. Do you mind taking me on an errand, first?" she asked. "It would be almost on our way—that is, if you're going to take me to that charming restaurant in the Bois that I've heard so much about. Are you?"

Barnes met her dancing eyes gravely. "I am, my dear, if you permit me. Where do we go first, then?"

"I just got word," and she indicated a letter on her dresser, "that some friends of the family are here. I must see them, just for a moment—just to introduce you, pay my respects, and arrange to see them tomorrow. They're in an apartment off the Avenue Mozart, in Auteuil. The address is 27, Bis, Rue Jasmin."

"That," said Barnes, "settles it."

"What do you mean?" she asked. "You don't mind stopping there?"

Barnes laughed a little, but behind the laughter his eyes were cold. He caught her by the shoulders, looked into her face.

"You're beautiful, my dear, beautiful!" he murmured. "The loveliest thing I've ever seen, I do believe—"

She yielded to him, her face lifted, her arms lowered. Then, swift as light, Barnes caught her two wrists, brought them behind her back, caught them together in one hand. From his cuff he jerked a handkerchief; even as her face changed, as a sharp little cry broke from her, he had the handkerchief knotted about her wrists. From his coat pocket he took a larger handkerchief, this time of silk. He wound it about her mouth, forced her jaws open, forced in the handkerchief, tied it securely.

She struggled furiously the while. She was helpless against

his strength, against the surprise of his attack. He forced her back violently into the depths of a chair, then uttered a sharp exclamation. Catching one shoulder of her filmy gown, he tore it away—to reveal, bedded against the silken covering of her breast, a tiny pistol. Barnes took the little weapon and pocketed it.

He paid no heed to the agonized, furious stare of her dilated eyes, to her incoherent sounds. From the corner he brought several towels, and tied her securely in the chair.

"You forget, my dear, that my life is far more important to me than your beauty, modesty or welfare," he observed, and glanced at the letter on the dresser. "No fake, eh? Your attention to detail is almost Teutonic, my dear young lady. Only one thing was wrong. When that fellow was killed in here, the wound in his head did not fit the projections at the foot of your bed. Next time, pay more attention to such things. *Au revoir!* I'll be back later."

He turned out the lights, locked the door, and departed—taking the key.

He left the hotel. A taxicab was to the right of the entrance; he heard the voice of Eramian, and went to it. He had brought the girl's letter.

"They were kind enough to write the address; here it is. Third B, at 27, Bis, Rue Jasmin. In Auteuil. Good luck! I'll be here after nine—you may come openly."

The taxi departed, with another in its wake. Barnes strode briskly onto the boulevards, hailing a cruising taxicab, and went to the Quai des Agustins.

There, he paid off the man a block from his destination, and approached this afoot. The Japanese curio shop was dark. Everything was dark. Barnes mounted the stairs and knocked softly at the door of Santos Fleurien, the music teacher. No answer. No light from beneath the door. He pressed hard, threw his weight on it; the ancient door gave.

All was dark. Barnes stepped in, remembering the big room

perfectly; then a laugh came to his lips. Why, of course! The pianist had gone to Rue Jasmin—he recollected the massive, burly fellow. Just the man for such work. So much the worse for him!

Crossing to the painting which he had tapped that afternoon, he took out his knife and attacked it. No time to seek the hidden door itself—the canvas would do. A long slit, and he ventured a look. A room, its walls hung with shelves, porcelains in evidence; Oriental, Japanese. Barnes slit the canvas further. The lighted room beyond was empty. Stairs to the left—descending to the curio shop, no doubt.

He held aside the canvas and stepped through. Somewhere a telephone rang. A voice responded, in the clipped syllables of a Japanese speaking French. A stroke of luck, this. Barnes crossed to a doorway hung with a curtain, pressed this slightly aside, looked into a larger room where a man sat at a desk. A gorgeous Oriental room. The man, a Japanese, was absorbed in his telephone conversation. A slim man, handsome, energetic. On the desk before him was a typewriter, on which he had been at work.

Barnes compressed his lips; then took from his pocket the pistol that was not a pistol. He lifted it and aimed steadily. There was slight sound, a "plop" as of compressed air. Something struck the typewriter, burst, and was gone—it was like the breaking of a capsule.

THE JAPANESE swung around, startled by the sound. Barnes dropped the curtain for a moment. Then he stole a look. The Japanese was trying to rise, clutching at his throat. He had replaced the telephone on its rack. Back into the chair fell the man.

Barnes hurried forward. The gas was swift and sure, but not lethal. After an hour, two hours, Baron Hayashi would recover; on the morrow he would be himself again. That is, if he still lived on the morrow. Japanese of his quality were not inclined to outlive a crushing defeat.

In his hip pocket, Barnes carried a protective mask of impregnated gauze sewed in a handkerchief; he had it out already, was knotting it about his mouth and nostrils as he advanced. It fitted snugly. One glance at the closely written report Hayashi had been making on the typewriter, at the two sheets already typed, and Barnes caught these up. Then he frisked the unconscious man.

Letters, notebook, thin rice-paper cables—everything went in a pile. He turned to the desk, shot open the drawers, went through them rapidly, thoroughly. The pile grew. An automatic, he laid close to hand; Hayashi was not alone in the place, obviously. On the floor was an open brief-case; into it Barnes stuffed everything that he found.

"Looks like a cleanup and no mistake," he reflected jubilantly.

For a moment he stooped above Baron Hayashi. When he rose, the olive forehead of the Japanese bore the scarlet insigne of the Sphinx, U. S. A. He looked at it, nodded—then heard a startled gasp.

He whirled, and in the same motion reached for the automatic. A curtain had been brushed aside. Another Japanese stood there, eyes distended—the same man who had been following him that morning. A pistol whipped up.

Barnes fired, the fraction of a second before the other shot rang out.

Two minutes later, he was stumbling down the studio stairs into the dark street where assistance awaited him.

CHAPTER VII

A MATTER OF HONOR

Ten minutes to nine.

Barnes flung open the door of his room at the hotel. Flandreau was there, awaiting him. He tossed his brief-case to the bed and looked down at his right hand. Blood was dripping from his fingers. Flandreau uttered a sharp exclamation and sprang forward.

"Thanks. Lend a hand, like a good chap," said Barnes coolly. "Hurts like hell."

He stripped off coat and shirt and revealed a double hurt. The bullet had ripped across his right arm, also across the ribs. An inch more to the left and the lung would have been punctured.

"No use asking questions, I suppose?" said Flandreau caustically, as he contrived a bandage from the bathroom medicine chest.

"Save your breath," and Barnes laughed.

"I've been trying to reach you for two hours. I've got those messages that Colonel d'Aleyne has decoded."

"Right. No time to lose. Help me into the shirt—thanks. Coat's ripped; won't be noticed. Damn that tie!" Barnes was working rapidly as he spoke. Shirt and collar, vest, coat, black tie. He whirled on the Frenchman. "Quick! The messages!"

Flandreau produced them. Barnes glanced at them. The one which he had first shown Colonel d'Aleyne was worked out in full:

Key: PALM.

E E T E K C X K I U 4 7 T K O U
T E X T O F G O L D A C C O R D

O B 6 P 6 J Q P F 4 I 5 A 5 6 0
S E N T B Y U S U A L M E A N S

Text of Gold Accord sent by usual means.

Barnes selected this from the others, put it in a separate pocket.

"We've got him," he said quietly. He motioned to the briefcase. "There's Hayashi's half-written code report to his government, letters, cables—everything he had. You and I will go through it a little later. You'll find interesting payment for your alliance with me. Satisfied?"

"*Mon Dieu!* Are you in earnest?" cried the amazed Frenchman. Barnes held up his arm.

"Does this look like a joke? That's not all. You may have to get some friends of mine out of jail in the morning—ah! That must be from them."

The telephone rang. He answered. It was Eramian.

"Three men there, *m'sieu'.* They remain. Two of us are hurt, not badly. Shall I come to the hotel? I think we got away unobserved."

"No. I don't need you, thanks. The usual place, tomorrow."

He glanced at Flandreau with a thin smile. "I fancy you'll not have to get 'em out of jail after all. You'll find a mess in Auteuil, however. I was to have been murdered there tonight. You'd best arrange to investigate everyone found there. However, we've other business on hand."

A STEP outside, a sharp tap on the door. Flandreau threw his hands and eyes to heaven, murmuring something about the accursed energy of these Americans. Barnes opened the door to admit Westlake, who was in correct evening attire, even to a high silk hat.

"Ah, come in, Westlake! Do you know Flandreau—no? Of the Sûreté. Sit down and make yourself comfortable. Very good of you to come."

Westlake bowed to Flandreau, and settled himself in a chair. He was cool, wary, with an urbane, polished air.

"By the way," he observed, "there's a charming girl from home at this hotel. I knew her family—she's over here to study music. I must look her up."

"Waste of time," said Barnes curtly.

Westlake's brows lifted. "Eh? I don't get you, old chap."

"What I mean is, you've got no time to waste," and Barnes handed him the separate decoded message. "Cast your eye over that."

Westlake did so. His features did not change. A slow, mortal pallor crept into them, but he did not flinch. His gaze lifted, puzzled, inquiring.

"Yes? I don't quite understand."

Barnes produced the other messages. "Look at these. The originals, in your writing, go to the Embassy in the morning. You may be aware that Baron von Bohm is under arrest; no? He coughed up everything. Anne Warren failed; she told everything. Baron Hayashi has told everything. Santos Fleurien and the two men with him can't tell; they're dead. Now, Mr. Benedict Arnold Junior, what about it?"

Westlake looked at the pistol in the hand of Barnes, Baron Hayashi's pistol. He put down the messages; his hand was steady. The pallor of his features had deepened to a livid hue.

"Apparently," he observed, and took a puff from his cigarette, "there's nothing for me to say."

"Your mistake." The voice of Barnes was crisp. "Mr. Flandreau, here, is just leaving; with you. He'll take you either to the Sûreté, if you prefer publicity and being turned over to the United States for trial; or else he'll accompany you to your apartment and leave you alone in your bedroom—for a few moments. Which?"

Westlake drew a deep breath.

"Very good of you," he said, "to give me the choice. I'd like to write a letter, yes, before I—retire. I appreciate the opportunity."

"Take this with you," and Barnes handed him the pistol, grimly. "And don't try any tricks; there'll be a dozen men watching you all the way home, and around your apartment house. Good-by. Flandreau, you don't mind? If you'll return here later, we'll split Baron Hayashi's stuff fifty-fifty."

Flandreau, who looked uncomfortable, bowed and departed with Westlake, silently.

A DEEP breath escaped Barnes. His shoulders sagged; in utter relaxation, the tension gone, he looked years older. He was suddenly weary, mentally weary. He moved over to the dresser, got out a bottle of whiskey, and poured a drink.

"Done!" he muttered, as he downed the liquor. "Done—all of it. A cleanup. Good God, how the Sphinx has struck—right and left, like a fiend! He'll be remembered for this night's work. They'll not try murder again in a hurry. Hayashi will commit suicide, or else get out. Westlake should go to Leavenworth; but he's better off dead, and a scandal avoided. We've got everything; we've wiped the slate clean. A great job!"

He sank into a chair, wiped sweat from his forehead. His hand, drifting to his pocket, touched something; a key. The key to Anne Warren's room. He sprang to his feet.

"Ah!" He hesitated at the door. "After all, she's a damned beautiful creature. Surely the Sphinx can pardon as well as strike—surely! Perhaps Westlake told the truth. Perhaps he did know her family in America; she must have lived there. Perhaps she and Westlake—ah!"

He started at the thought. Could that be it? Had she persuaded Westlake to his course of treachery? A handsome fellow,

Westlake. A lovely girl, this. A smile, half of pity, touched his lips. He put out his hand to the door.

"Yes. Let the Sphinx be kind, be merciful—for once."

And he was gone toward the girl's room.

H . BEDFORD-JONES

BEDFORD-JONES IS a Canadian by birth, but not by profession, having removed to the United States at the age of one year. For over twenty years he has been more or less profitably engaged in writing and traveling. As he has seldom resided in one place longer than a year or so and is a person of retiring habits, he is somewhat a man of mystery; more than once he has suffered from unscrupulous gentlemen who impersonated him—one of whom murdered a wife and was subsequently shot by the police, luckily after losing his alias.

The real Bedford-Jones is an elderly man, whose gray hair and precise attire give him rather the appearance of a retired foreign diplomat. His hobby is stamp collecting, and his collection of Japan is said to be one of the finest in existence. At present writing he is en route to Morocco, and when this appears in print he will probably be somewhere on the Mojave Desert in company with Erle Stanley Gardner.

Questioned as to the main facts in his life, he declared there was only one main fact, but it was not for publication; that his life had been uneventful except for numerous financial losses, and that his only adventures lay in evading adventurers. In his younger years he was something of an athlete, but the encroachments of age preclude any active pursuits except that of motoring. He is usually to be found poring over his stamps, working at his typewriter, or laboring in his California rose garden, which is one of the sights of Cathedral Cañon, near Palm Springs.

Bedford-Jones has written stories laid in many corners of the earth, but among his most popular tales were the John Solomon stories which started many years ago in the *Argosy*.